Rochelle Kao.
23rd Dec 07
KL.

The Pig With Green Spots

and

Other Stories

by
ENID BLYTON

Illustrated by

Diana Catchpole

AWARD PUBLICATIONS

For further information on Enid Blyton please visit
www.blyton.com

ISBN-10: 1-84135-435-X
ISBN-13: 978-1-84135-435-4

First published by Sampson Low as *Enid Blyton's Holiday
Book Series*

This edition entitled *The Pig with Green Spots and Other Stories*
published by permission of Enid Blyton Limited

First published by Award Publications Limited 1993
This edition first published 2005
Second impression 2007

Published by Award Publications Limited,
The Old Riding School, The Welbeck Estate,
Worksop, Nottinghamshire, S80 3LR

Printed in Singapore

CONTENTS

The Pig
With Green Spots

There was once a pig with big green spots all over his fat body. He stood on the mantelpiece next to the clock. He was made of china, and fitted underneath him was a little place to lock and unlock him, because he was a money-box.

He had a curly tail and two pointed ears, and he really was very ugly indeed. Nobody knew why he had been made bright pink with green spots. They just thought he was terrible.

He belonged to old Mrs Loveday. She used him as a money-box and he was quite full. He had a slit in his back to put copper and silver coins, and now that he was full he felt very heavy.

When Lucy came to see old Mrs

5

Loveday, she always looked at the pig with green spots, standing next to the clock on the mantelpiece. She really couldn't bear him. She said she didn't like the way he looked at her, and she didn't like the big spots all over him.

"He looks as if he's got an illness," she told her mother. "I wish Mrs Loveday wouldn't have him. He's ugly."

One day Lucy went to see Mrs Loveday by herself. Mummy had taken little brother James further on in the pram. She was going to call for Lucy when she came back. Lucy knocked at Mrs Loveday's old wooden door. But nobody said "Come in".

She turned the handle and the door opened. Lucy walked right in. Mrs Loveday always told her to do that. Lucy liked walking right in. There was no hall in old Mrs Loveday's house. You walked straight into the spotless little kitchen.

Mrs Loveday was out in her garden hanging up clothes. Lucy looked round the room. It was a funny little room, with red geraniums on the window-sill, a little rocking-chair by the fireplace, a small yellow stool that Lucy liked to sit on – and, of course, the pig with green spots was on the mantelpiece, as usual.

"I shan't look at him," said Lucy to herself. "I don't like him."

She sat down on the little yellow stool and looked at the clock. It had stopped. Lucy thought it would be a good idea to wind it up. Mrs Loveday liked to have little jobs like that done for her. So Lucy stood up and took down the clock. She wound it up carefully.

She reached up to the mantelpiece to put it back – and then a dreadful thing happened. The clock knocked against the china pig – and the pig fell right off the mantelpiece into the fender below!

It smashed into a hundred pieces. They flew everywhere, into every corner – tiny bits of bright pink china, some of them with green spots on them.

The money fell out of the pig too. Silver and copper coins rolled here and there, into the fender, under the sofa,

8

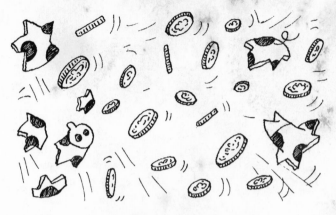

over the rug – there seemed to be dozens and dozens of them.

Lucy stood and stared in horror. Look at that now – the pig was quite smashed, and all the money was spilt. Whatever would Mrs Loveday say? She must like the pig very much or she would never have had him on her mantelpiece for so long.

Lucy was frightened. She didn't want to tell Mrs Loveday. After all, nobody had seen her come in. Why couldn't she slip out and go and meet Mummy? She could tell her that Mrs Loveday wasn't there. Nobody would know she had been into the kitchen and broken the pig.

9

Lucy crept to the door. But even as she put her hand on the latch, she stopped.

No – she simply couldn't run away! She had broken something by accident, and she must say so. Even if Mrs Loveday and Mummy didn't know, and needn't ever know, she herself, little Lucy, would know, and would feel ashamed of herself for running away. Mummy always said you must never run away from anything.

"But it's awfully hard to stay," said poor Lucy to herself, as she stood and looked at the pig. "Oh dear – here comes Mrs Loveday!"

Old Mrs Loveday came trotting in.

She cried out in delight when she saw the little girl waiting for her.

"Well, I never! If it isn't Lucy come along to see me again!"

Lucy looked at Mrs Loveday and didn't smile. "Please," she said, "I've done something dreadful. I broke your money-box pig!"

Mrs Loveday looked down at the broken pieces and all the money. Lucy waited to be scolded. But to her enormous surprise Mrs Loveday laughed.

"Bless us all! So that ugly pig is broken at last, and I can get the money out of him. You know, Lucy, I lost the key ages ago, and couldn't get out my money. I didn't like to break the pig, because my sister gave him to me years ago. But I'm glad to see such an ugly creature go, and to get my money. You *have* done me a good turn!"

"Have I really?" said Lucy, smiling all over her face in delight. "Oh, I was so afraid of staying to tell you, Mrs Loveday!"

11

"Never be afraid of telling a thing you've done," said the old woman, beginning to sweep up the bits. "I think all the more of you for being brave and good. Yes, so I do! And, you see, I'm glad of the accident because I badly wanted some money today. My granddaughter's coming to see me, and I want to bake a big cake for her. I'll take some of this money and go and buy some flour and currants and chocolate and butter! Ah, I'll make a fine cake!"

"Lucy! I've come back for you!" suddenly called Mummy's voice, from outside the gate. Lucy said goodbye to old Mrs Loveday and ran off. She had picked up all the money she could see, and there was such a lot piled on the table for Mrs Loveday.

That afternoon Lucy went by Mrs Loveday's house again, and the old lady saw her. "Lucy! My cake is lovely. You *must* have a nice big slice to take home to tea! Here it is! Doesn't the mantelpiece look nice without that ugly pig, with his green spots?"

"Yes, it does," said Lucy. "Thank you for the cake, Mrs Loveday. I shall enjoy it!"

She did, and as she ate it she told Mummy all about the pink pig. Mummy was pleased.

"You're a good girl," she said. "And how nice it is to sit here eating this delicious cake, knowing that you got it because you were brave enough to stay and own up. Really, I'm very pleased with you, Lucy."

"I feel pleased too," said Lucy. "I shall never be a coward now. It's much nicer to be brave!"

I Certainly Didn't

It all began one morning when Dame Click's little grandson, Rolly, let his ball go over the wall into Mr Shouter's garden. That wouldn't have mattered much if only Mr Shouter hadn't been sitting in his deck-chair, fast asleep and dreaming, exactly underneath the falling ball.

The ball fell bang on Mr Shouter's head and in his dreams he thought a bomb had fallen on him – and he woke up, trembling and afraid.

But when he saw that it was only a ball that had hit him he jumped up in a tremendous rage. He saw Rolly's head sticking up over the wall, and he let out a tremendous roar. Rolly was frightened and slid back into his grandmother's garden.

"You bad boy! You wicked little scamp!" yelled Mr Shouter. "Throwing a ball at a sleeping old man! I'm coming over to smack you – and I've got the hardest hand in Cheer-Up Village!"

Mr Shouter had a very loud voice. Rolly ran into Dame Click's house and hid behind the dresser in the kitchen. Mr Shouter jumped straight over the wall and came after him.

"I'll put you in the wash-tub!" he shouted when he saw poor trembling Rolly. "I'll iron you out flat! I'll peg you up on the line! I'll beat you like a carpet. I'll –"

Dame Click bustled into the kitchen, quite alarmed. When she saw Mr

Shouter she shooed him as if he was a cat.

"Shoo! Go away! Shoo! Shoo!"

"Stop shooing me!" yelled Mr Shouter. "I've come to get that grandson of yours! Hitting me on the head with his ball!"

"Did you do that on purpose, Rolly?" demanded Dame Click.

"I certainly didn't!" said Rolly from behind the dresser. "It was quite an accident. I was just looking over the wall to say I was sorry, when –"

"You did it on purpose! You're a bad boy, a wicked scamp!" began Mr Shouter all over again. He grabbed at Rolly and a jug fell off the dresser on to his big foot. Then how Mr Shouter leapt around on one leg, shouting and holding his hurt foot!

"Serves you right for losing your temper!" said Dame Click. "Shoo!"

"If you shoo me again I'll turn you into a hedgehog, you prickly old woman!" cried Mr Shouter.

"Now, that's enough!" said Dame Click, and picking up a broom, she

swept round Mr Shouter's feet as if she was sweeping him up! How angry he was!

"You wait!" he said. "You wait! As soon as I get back I'll look up my magic books and I'll work some magic that will make you very, very, sorry. You wait! You'll be surprised at some of the things that will happen to you today!"

"Shoo!" said Dame Click, and swept him up again. He went off to his own house, muttering and grumbling. Old Mr Shouter had a very hot temper indeed!

"Now, don't you let your ball go into Mr Shouter's garden any more," said Dame Click to Rolly.

17

"I can't. It's still in his garden and I guess he won't throw it over now," said poor Rolly, scrambling out from behind the dresser. "Are you soon going out, Gran? I'll go with you."

Now Dame Click had her little granddaughter staying with her, too. She was only a year old and she went out in a big pram. Dame Click sat her in it and put a rug over her, for it was a cold morning. Then she and Rolly and little Susie set out for the village shops.

Mr Shouter also set out, carrying a basket. Dame Click saw him and kept carefully out of his way. She didn't want any shouting in the middle of the village street!

She came to the market-place. Rolly loved that. There was always such a lot going on. Hens clucked, ducks quacked, old countrywomen sat on tubs to sell butter and eggs, rhubarb and early lettuces.

"Now," said Dame Click, "I'll put the pram just here, where it will be safe. You come with me, Rolly, because I'm going to buy a nice lot of things and you can take them back to the pram for me and put them under Susie's rug."

So off they went, leaving Susie fast asleep in her pram.

Dame Click bought a great many things. She bought a fat chicken, ready for cooking. She bought a beautiful new red shawl for herself. She bought a silver bowl for Susie to eat her porridge from, and she bought a pair of blue shoes for Rolly. She gave them all to him.

"Now run back to the pram and pop them into it," she said. "Under the rug, mind – and don't you wake Susie!" Rolly ran off, and Dame Click began to talk to a friend of hers. When she had had a good chat, she went off to find Rolly and Susie and the pram. Susie was still in the pram, fast asleep. But Rolly was nowhere to be seen.

Dame Click caught sight of Mr Shouter at the next stall. "Ah! I expect Rolly saw him and ran off home," she thought. "Bad-tempered old man! Telling me he'll work magic on me like that! Pooh! Bah!"

She lifted up the rug to put in a loaf of

bread she had bought – and, my goodness me, how she stared. Where was her fat chicken? Where was the red shawl? And what had become of the silver bowl and the blue shoes? In the pram was a smelly old bone, a ragged red duster, a broken dish and a pair of holey old shoes. Dame Click gaped at them and then she gave a loud cry.

"It's that horrid old Mr Shouter! He's worked bad magic on me as he said he would. He's changed my chicken into a bone, my shawl into a red rag, the silver bowl into a cracked dish, and the blue shoes into a broken-down pair! Oh, the wicked old man!"

People heard her crying out and came to hear. She pointed to Mr Shouter and said it all over again. "Where's Mr Clop, the policeman? Fetch him at once."

Mr Clop came with his notebook. "What's the matter, what's the matter?" he said sternly.

"It's Mr Shouter," said Dame Click. "See what he's done to me! He's changed my chicken into a bone, my –"

"I certainly didn't!" said Mr Shouter in a loud voice.

"And my red shawl into a rag and my –"

"I CERTAINLY DIDN'T!" said Mr Shouter in a still louder voice.

"Well, if you didn't, you've taken them then, you bad fellow!" said Dame Click, and she began to cry. "Arrest him, Mr Clop. He said he would work bad magic on me and he has."

"I know I said that – but I was in a temper and I didn't really mean it," said Mr Shouter, looking worried.

"You'd better come along with me," said Mr Clop, and he walked off with Mr Shouter. Everyone said comforting words to Dame Click. To think she had spent so much money and then had all her things changed into rubbish! She went home, wheeling the pram. Susie was still asleep. When she got home the kitchen door was open and Rolly was sitting at the table, playing with a puzzle – and, dear me, what were all those things on the floor beside him?

Dame Click's eyes nearly fell out of
her head. Yes – a fat chicken ready for
cooking – a beautiful red shawl – a silver
bowl – and a fine pair of small blue
shoes! She gave a gulp and sank down
into a chair.

"Rolly! Where did those come from?"

"Why, Gran, you gave them to me
yourself!" said Rolly in surprise. "But I
didn't like to put them into the pram as
you told me to, because old Mr Shouter
was nearby. So I brought them home
instead."

"Oh my, oh my, and I've sent Mr
Shouter off to the police-station with Mr
Clop!" said Dame Click in dismay. "But
how did all those awful things come to
be in my pram?"

23

"Awful things? What awful things?" asked Rolly. "Oh those! Well, Gran, my friend came along – Pippy, you know – and he was taking the bone to his dog, the rag was for polishing up his bicycle, the cracked dish was to be mended and he was going to give the old shoes to the tramp at the crossroads. But he wanted to go and play football with the other boys so he put them into the pram for a few minutes."

"This is terrible," said Dame Click. "Who would have thought of such a thing! Take the things to Pippy at once, Rolly. Oh my, oh my, now I must go to the police-station and fetch back Mr Shouter!"

So off she went, wheeling the pram with Susie in it, still fast asleep. When she got to the police-station Mr Clop was shouting at Mr Shouter and Mr Shouter was yelling at Mr Clop. "I tell you I didn't, I certainly didn't!" yelled Mr Shouter. "As if I'd do a thing like that! Changing all those nice things into rubbish! I CERTAINLY DIDN'T!"

"Oh, Mr Clop, it's all a mistake! Oh, Mr Shouter, do forgive me!" said poor Dame Click, and she did her best to explain, though she was very much afraid that Mr Shouter would turn her into a black beetle.

But he didn't. He began to laugh. Then he patted Dame Click on the shoulder. "Funniest thing I've heard for a long time!" he said. "Ho, ho! So Pippy put all that rubbish there!"

"Hmmm," said Mr Clop, annoyed that all the notes he had put down in his book were of no use after all. "Hmmm, I've a good mind to arrest you, Dame Click, for Making a Fuss about Nothing!"

Dame Click squealed and rushed out of the police-station as if a hundred

25

tigers were after her. Mr Shouter laughed and went with her.

"Oh, Mr Shouter – I'm so sorry," stammered Dame Click. "Such a lot of foolishness. I suppose you wouldn't come in and have a piece of my chocolate cake, would you – and a sip of my lemonade? Just to show there's no ill-feeling."

"I certainly will!" said Mr Shouter, and went to her cottage with her. As soon as Rolly saw him he got behind the dresser again – but how he stared when he saw his gran and Mr Shouter sitting down to eat chocolate cake and drink lemonade. And will you believe it, in half a minute he was on Mr Shouter's knee, eating chocolate cake, too!

What a storm in a tea-cup! Everything is peaceful now – but just wait till that rascal of a Rolly lets something else go over the wall!

The Tin Whistle

Paul had a tin-whistle that had a very loud whistle indeed. His mother got very tired of it. "Paul! If you don't stop blowing that whistle I shall take it away and put it into the dustbin!" she cried.

"Oh no, Mother!" said Paul in alarm. "It's the best one I've ever had."

"Well, go into the woods and play there," said Mother. "You can whistle all you like there, for there is no one to hear you! Maybe the birds will get a bit tired of you, but they can always fly away, and I can't!"

So Paul went to the woods with his tin-whistle. He blew it and he blew it, and at last he had no breath left.

"I'll climb a tree and have a rest," he

said. "It shall be my ship, swaying on the sea."

So he climbed a big tree and sat near the top, swaying in the wind, for all the world like a ship bobbing to and fro on the sea.

After a while he got out his tin-whistle and looked at it. "I think I shall be the guard of a train now," he said. "The tree is the train. When I blow my whistle the train must go!"

But before he blew his whistle again, he heard voices. They were the voices of two boys. Paul peeped down to the bottom of the tree. The boys were standing underneath, talking.

"Now, I'll creep through the hedge into Farmer Brown's strawberry field with my basket," said one boy, "and you stay here and keep watch for me. You can see the road well from here. If you see anyone coming, whistle. See? Then I shall hear your whistle and come back before I'm caught. We'll share whatever strawberries I get."

"Oooh, the naughty bad boys!"

thought Paul, shocked. "Those are my daddy's strawberries. Those boys mean to steal them! What shall I do? If I climb down and tell them to go away, they will fight me and knock me down. But I can't stay here and see Daddy's fruit stolen!"

The first boy was already creeping through the hedge with his basket. The other boy was standing beneath the tree, watching the road, which could be seen clearly from where he stood.

Then Paul had a marvellous idea. He put his tin-whistle to his mouth and blew hard. Pheeeeeeeee!

29

The boy who was climbing through the hedge at once squeezed back again, and ran to join his friend in the wood.

"Is there somebody coming?" he asked. "I heard your whistle."

"Well, I didn't whistle," said the other boy, puzzled.

"You must have!" said the first boy. "I heard you!"

"Well *I* heard a whistle too, but it wasn't *me* whistling," said his friend. "Go on – try again. No one's coming."

Paul let the boy get right into the field, then he blew on his whistle again: Pheeeeeeeee! Pheeeeeeeee! At once the

boy scrambled back through the hedge and ran helter-skelter into the wood. "You whistled again!" he panted. "Who's coming?"

"Nobody. And I didn't whistle, and I can't think who did!" said the second boy angrily, looking all round. "Perhaps it was a bird."

"It *was* you whistling!" said the other boy. "I know your whistle. You are just playing tricks on me."

"No, I'm not," said the second boy. "Go on – try again."

But as soon as the boy got into the field, Paul whistled even more loudly than before: Pheeeeeeeee! Pheeeeeeeee! PHEE!

Back came the boy, panting. "That *was* your whistle!" he cried. "Is there anyone coming?"

"No, there isn't, and it *wasn't* my whistle I tell you," said the boy, half afraid, looking all round him. "Whoever can be whistling here?"

Then Paul thought he would try a big deep voice and see what would happen. So he said in a growly, fierce voice: "BAD BOYS! WICKED BOYS! I CAN SEE YOU! WAIT TILL I CATCH YOU!"

"Oh! Oh! It's the farmer!" cried the boys, and they ran off through the wood at top speed, leaving their basket behind them. Paul blew a long blast on his whistle and climbed down the tree. He picked up the basket and went home to tell his mother what had happened, blowing his whistle hard all the time.

"Paul! Stop!" cried his mother. "That dreadful whistle!"

"Well, just listen what it did!" said Paul proudly, and he told his mother how the whistle had saved his father's strawberries. How his mother laughed! She was very pleased.

"That was clever of you, Paul," she said. "Well, well! As it's such a smart whistle I suppose I'll have to let you blow it as much as you like. Blow away!"

"No, I won't annoy you, Mother!" said Paul. "I'll only blow it loudly in the woods. And maybe it will scare some more strawberry thieves away. I shouldn't be at all surprised."

And neither should I!

He Never
Knew the Time

Goofy never seemed to know the time! If his mother said to him, "Be home at five o'clock for tea, Goofy!" he would arrive at six.

And if she said, "Now be sure to catch the twelve o'clock bus," he would arrive at quarter past and find it was gone.

Goofy could tell the time all right. He knew perfectly well what the clock said. But he never thought of keeping an eye on the time, as we all have to do if we are to be early and not late for everything.

Goofy's mother got very cross with him. "I'm tired of telling you to be home by this time and that, and reminding you to catch the right bus and the right train, and to be at the school at the right time," she said. "I'm really tired of it. I shan't tell you any more."

"Oh, Mother! Do you suppose I shall get worse and worse?" said Goofy, in alarm. "I just can't seem to keep an eye on the time, as you are always telling me to."

"Well," said his mother, an idea coming into her head very suddenly. "Well, if you can't keep an *eye* on the time, maybe you could keep an *ear*, Goofy!"

"An ear? What do you mean, Mother?" asked Goofy in surprise.

"I'll show you," said his mother, and took down the clock from the kitchen

mantelpiece. "Now see, Goofy – this is my alarm clock. You know that it rings a bell very loudly, at whatever time I set this little hand to, don't you?"

"Yes," said Goofy, still puzzled. "I know you set that little tiny hand at six, and exactly at six the bell rings and wakens you up."

"Right," said his mother. "Well, Goofy, I want you to be home at half past twelve today because the dinner is hot. So I am setting this little hand at a quarter past twelve – do you see? The bell will ring loudly then, and you will

36

hear it. And straightaway you will come home and be here in time to wash your hands and sit down to your hot dinner at half past twelve."

"Oh!" said Goofy, surprised. "I hope the others won't laugh at me, Mother."

"I expect they will," said his mother. "But, as I said before, Goofy, if I can't make you keep an eye on the time, I can at least make you keep an ear on it!"

Goofy put the clock into a bag and went out to meet his friends. He set the bag down on the seat where they all put their coats and other belongings and began to play very happily. One child went off at twelve o'clock, and another just after. They kept their eyes on the time and left just when they ought to.

37

But Goofy as usual didn't keep his eyes on the time at all. He went on playing with the others, thinking that he still had at least half the morning left. Then suddenly the alarm went off in the bag.

"R-r-r-r-r-ring! R-r-r-r-r-ring!"

Everyone jumped. "What's that?" they cried and ran to look. "R-r-r-r-r-ring!" went the kitchen clock, loudly. "R-r-r-r-r-ring!"

"Gosh! It's an alarm clock!" said the children laughing. "Oh, Goofy – has your mother given you an alarm clock to tell you the time to go home!"

"Nothing to laugh at!" said Goofy, going red. "Just a good idea, that's all. I must go. It's a quarter past twelve."

He was sitting down to his hot dinner, with his hands washed and his hair brushed, at exactly half past twelve. His mother was very pleased. She took the clock and set it for two o'clock.

"I want you to catch the ten past two bus to Granny's," she said, "and take her these apples."

At two o'clock Goofy was playing happily with his trains on the floor. The clock suddenly rang loudly and Goofy jumped.

"R-r-r-r-ring! R-r-ring!"

"All right, all right," said Goofy. "Don't shout so loudly. I can hear you."

His mother said goodbye to him, and set the clock for half past five. "You can have tea with Granny and be home about six," she said. "Put the clock in your school satchel. That's right."

Granny got quite a shock when the clock rang out its alarm loudly at half past five.

"R-r-r-ring!" it said. "R-r-r-r-r-ring!"

"What in the world is that noise?" said Granny. "It can't be the telephone.

And it certainly isn't any of the door-
bells."

"It's the alarm clock in my satchel,"
said Goofy, going red.

"But why do you keep an alarm clock
in your satchel?" said Granny, in
surprise. "What a funny thing to do!
You really are a silly boy, Goofy."

"It's just so that I can keep an ear on
the time," said Goofy. "Don't laugh at
me, Granny."

But Granny did laugh. She really
couldn't help it. She made Goofy stop
the clock ringing and then he put on his
coat to go home.

The next day his mother set the clock
for half past twelve. Goofy was to go to
school that day, and he came out at a

quarter past. But he played on the way home and was always late for his dinner.

"Now, the clock is set for half past twelve, Goofy," said his mother. "As soon as it goes off it will remind you that you must come home at once or you will be late. No playing on the way home today!"

Goofy came out from school at twenty past twelve. He went with the other boys to a little stream and they all began to throw stones into the water.

Goofy forgot all about the time – but the alarm clock didn't! It was in his satchel on the bank, and it suddenly trilled out loudly.

"R-r-r-ring! R-r-r-r-r-r-ring! R-r-r-r-r-ring!"

"What's that?" said the boys, startled. Goofy ran to his bag and stopped the ringing.

"He's got an alarm clock in his bag!" cried Peter. "Oh, what fun! Poor old Goofy, he never remembers the time, so he has to carry an alarm clock about with him." How the boys teased poor Goofy!

How they laughed at him! He didn't like it at all. He went home at once, very red in the face, and rather angry.

"Mother," he said, when he got in. "Mother, I'm not going to carry that silly alarm clock about any more. Everyone laughs at me."

"Well, I'm sorry, dear," said his mother, "but I'm afraid you must. It's a wonderful idea. I've never known you so nice and punctual as you have been these last two days."

"Mother, *please* don't make me carry the clock about," said Goofy, almost in tears.

"Well, there's only one other way of getting you to be punctual instead of

42

always late," said his mother, "and you know very well you can't manage that other way."

"What is the other way?" asked Goofy.

"I've told you before," said his mother. "Either you keep an eye on the time, or an ear. You couldn't keep an eye on it, so I made you keep an ear on it."

"Oh, Mother – let me try to keep an eye on it now, please do," begged Goofy. "I really will try. I can't bear to carry the clock about with me any more! You can't imagine how the children laugh at me when the alarm goes off."

"I *can* imagine it," said his mother. "It makes me want to laugh myself. Well – shall I try you, Goofy? But I warn you, if you can't keep an eye on the time and come home at the right time, you'll have to take the clock again."

So now Goofy is doing his best to keep an eye on the time and he hasn't done badly so far! Are you good at keeping an eye on the time? You'd better be careful, in case you are made to keep an ear on it, too, like Goofy!

The Train That
Wouldn't Stop

In the nursery of the Princess Marigold
was a toy train. It was a very fine one
indeed. It was made of wood, painted all
colours. It didn't run on lines; it
trundled wherever it liked, round and
round the nursery.

It was rather a magic train. In the cab
of the red engine was a little knob.
When Princess Marigold pressed the
knob, the train began to run along,
pulling the carriages behind in a long
string. And it would go on running until
the princess said the word
"Hattikattikooli."

Then the train would stop suddenly
and stand absolutely still until the knob
in the engine's cab was once again
pressed.

44

Marigold had great fun with the train. She sat all her dolls and toys in it, pressed the knob, and off they went, trundling up and down. Sometimes she opened the door of her nursery and the train would rattle all down the passage and back, startling the king very much if he met it suddenly round a corner.

Now there were two small pixies who lived just outside the palace walls in a pansy bed. They were Higgle and Tops, and *how* they loved that little toy train. One day they climbed up the ivy, right up the wall, and in at the princess's window to see the train running.

They sat hidden behind a big doll on the window-sill, watching for the train to start.

Marigold put her rabbit into the cab of the engine to drive it. She put all the Noah's Ark animals into two of the carriages, her pink doll and teddy bear in the next one, and all the skittles in the rest. Higgle and Tops nearly fell off the window-sill trying to see what she did to start up the engine.

"She pressed a little knob!" whispered Higgle into Top's ear, making him jump. "She did! That's how you start it!"

"I know. I saw," said Tops. "Oh, Higgle, if only the princess would go out of the room for a bit we could have a ride in that train!"

And will you believe it, somebody called Marigold at that moment, and she ran out of the room, closing the door behind her in case the train ran out.

In a moment Higgle and Tops were down on the floor, running across to the moving train. Higgle got hold of the rabbit. "Get out!" he cried. "You can't

drive for toffee! Let *me* drive!"

The rabbit pushed Higgle away. The pink doll began to shout. The bear tried to get out of his carriage to go to the rabbit's help. When Tops began to pull at the rabbit, too, he just had to fall off the engine. Then Higgle and Tops leapt into the cab and began to drive. Oh, how lovely!

They drove round and round the nursery at such a tremendous speed that three of the skittles fell out, and the kangaroo in one of the front carriages was frightened and jumped out in a hurry.

"Stop!" called the pink doll. "You'll smash us all up! Stop, I tell you!" But Higgle and Tops had never driven a

47

train before in their lives and weren't
going to stop! No, they went faster and
faster and faster. And when Marigold
came back she was horrified to see her
little train tearing by like a mad thing
with all the toys hanging on for dear life
and shouting in fright.

"Hattikattikooli!" she cried, and the
train stopped so suddenly that everyone
was shot into the air, and fell in a heap
on the hearthrug. The pixies shot out,
too, and ran behind the dolls' house to
hide. They were trembling with
excitement.

"Bunny!" said Marigold, sternly,
looking round for the indignant rabbit.
"Bunny! Is *that* how you drive the train
when I am out of the room? For
shame!"

Behind the dolls' house there was a

little mousehole. Higgle nudged Tops. "Look! A mousehole! We'd better get down it before the toys come after us. They'll be dreadfully angry."

So down the mousehole they both crept. It was very small, and they had to crawl on their tummies – but, goodness me, it led right to the garden! That *was* a bit of luck for Higgle and Tops.

When the toys came to look for them behind the dolls' house, meaning to give them a really hard smacking for their naughtiness, they were not there.

"Just wait!" the rabbit shouted down the mousehole. "Just wait, you two! Next time you come we'll give you such a smacking!"

Higgle and Tops talked and talked about the train. How lovely it was to

49

drive! If only it was theirs! What long journeys they could go! What adventures they could have!

"Let's borrow it," said Higgle, at last. "Tops, we simply *must* drive it again. Let's go tonight and get it. We can creep up the mousehole. We know how to start it. Do let's."

"I'd love to," said Tops at once. "Oh, Higgle! Think of driving that train up and down hill, all across the countryside and everywhere!"

Well, that night the two of them went up the mousehole again, and into the nursery. The train was standing quietly in the corner. The toys were all at the other end, dancing to the musical-box. The rabbit was turning the handle, and nobody was looking round at all.

"Now's our chance!" whispered Higgle, and the two pixies made a rush for the train. They got into the cab, pressed the knob – and off they went!

The toys stopped dancing in fright and surprise.

The train rushed by them and out of

the open nursery door. Gracious! Where could it be going?

"It's those pixies! They've taken our train! How dare they!" cried the pink doll in a rage. But there was nothing to be done about it. The train was gone. It flew down the passage, bumped down a hundred stairs, ran to the garden door – and out it went into the garden!

"Here we go!" yelled Higgle, in delight. "Where to? We don't know and we don't care! Go on, train, go on, faster, faster, faster!"

All that night the train sped over fields and hills, through valleys and towns. When the dawn came, it turned to go back. Higgle and Tops had no idea at all where they were. They were just enjoying going faster and faster. The train hurried back over the hills and fields.

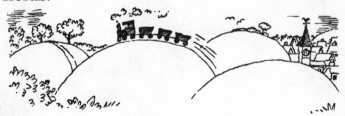

51

"I say – look!" said Higgle, suddenly. Tops looked – and there, not very far in front of them, were two red goblins, fighting hard. The pixies were very frightened indeed of goblins.

"Stop the train," said Higgle. "We don't want the goblins to see it. They'll catch it for their own."

"I can't remember the word to stop it," said Tops. "You said it, Higgle."

But Higgle couldn't remember it either! Oh, dear! Now they would never be able to stop the train! It flew on towards the fighting, yelling goblins, and knocked them both flat on their

backs. The pixies just had time to see an open sack filled with shining jewels as they passed. Then the train shot into a cave, bumping against the wall, buried itself in the earth and stopped with a shudder and a sigh. Its wheels went round still, but the train didn't move. It couldn't!

Higgle and Tops were thrown out. They sat in the dark cave trembling. They didn't dare to go out, in case the goblins saw them.

Outside, the shouting still went on. "You knocked me flat!" cried one goblin to another. "Take that– and that – and that!"

The second goblin howled. "Don't! Don't! I'll go away now, really I will. You can have everything yourself."

There was the sound of running footsteps. One of the goblins had gone. "Oho!" said the other. "He's gone. Well, I shall hide all the goods and keep guard over them. He may come back. I don't trust him!"

Higgle and Tops were sitting in the middle of the cave, still trembling, when something hit them hard. They jumped. Goodness, it was a glittering necklace! The goblin must have thrown it into the cave.

"A necklace!" whispered Higgle. "A real beauty! Where have they stolen it from?"

Blip! A ring hit Tops and another hit Higgle on the shoulder. Then came a shower of jewellery, falling all about the cave – thud, blip, crash! It soon looked like a treasure-cave, and Higgle and Tops didn't know where to go to avoid being hit as the goblin threw everything into the cave to hide it.

"My word!" whispered Tops at last. "I believe all this belongs to the Queen herself, Princess Marigold's mother. Imagine it, Higgle! Those goblins must have broken in and stolen all this last night."

"Well – how are we to get it back to the palace?" asked Higgle. "Look outside there – the goblin is sitting at the entrance to this cave, guarding his treasure. We'll never get past him carrying all this. He'd catch us at once."

"We can't stay here for ever though," said Tops. "It's cold and uncomfortable – and I'm getting hungry. Think of something, Higgle. Use your brains!"

"Use yours!" said Higgle. So they sat and thought and the only noise in the cave was the sound of the train wheels still going round and round, though the train couldn't move.

"*I* know!" said Higgle at last. "Let's pull the train out of the earth it's buried in, and go out in that. We can pile the jewels in the carriages."

"And they'll all be jerked out, silly!" said Tops.

"I'll tell you what we'll do!" said Higgle, getting excited. "We'll wind all the necklaces and bracelets and chains round the wheels. They'll keep on then. And we'll drop the rings down the engine funnel. They'll stay in there all right. Come on, Tops!"

They set to work. They wound the shining necklaces and bracelets and chains round and round the wheels. Then they dropped all the rings down the funnel. The train looked very pretty indeed when they had finished with it.

"I guess a train was never dressed up like this before!" said Higgle, pleased. "Now come on, Tops – help me to pull it out of this earth. Steady on! Jump in as soon as we've got it free, because it will shoot out of the cave at top speed. It's still going, you know! We haven't thought of the word to stop the wheels turning yet!"

At last they got the engine out of the earth, and it stood upright. The wheels turned swiftly. Higgle and Tops jumped into the cab just as the train began to move. It went twice round the cave and then shot out of the entrance full speed ahead, its wheels glittering and gleaming in the morning sun.

How it shone with all its jewels! The goblin stared open-mouthed at this sudden, extraordinary appearance of

what looked to him like a glittering snake.

The train rushed over his legs and made him yell. Before he could grab it, it disappeared, shining brilliantly. The pixies laughed. "That was a fine idea of ours. We've escaped with all the jewels without being caught!"

The train didn't need to be told to go to the palace. It longed to be home! It shot off and soon came to the garden. It couldn't find any door open and raced up and down the paths like a mad thing. The King and Queen saw it and stared in amazement as it ran by them.

"What is it? It's all shining and glittering," said the King. "It's as bright as those lovely jewels of yours that were stolen during the night, my love!"

Princess Marigold appeared. "Mother! Did you know my magic train was stolen? It's gone!"

At that moment the train shot back again up the path, shining brilliantly with the jewels round all its wheels. Marigold gave a squeal.

"Hattikattikooli! Hattikattikooli!"

Thankfully the train stopped just by her. She knelt down and looked at the wheels. "Mother! It's brought back all your stolen jewels! Do look!"

Higgle and Tops got out of the engine and bowed. "We brought them back to you," said Higgle grandly. "The two goblins stole them and hid them in a cave."

"Dear me – how very clever and brave of you," said the Queen, pleased. "You shall have a reward. I will give you a sackful of gold all for yourselves."

"Thank you, Madam!" said the pixies, beaming. Now they would be rich. "We

59

will take the train back to the nursery for you when you have taken all your jewels from the wheels and the funnel."

They ran it back to the nursery, feeling very pleased with themselves. The toys gazed at them in rage. Those pixies! They had taken the train all night!

"Good morning," said Higgle, stepping out. "We have an adventure to tell you. Listen!"

He told them all that had happened. The toys listened. "And," said Higgle at the end, "as a reward for bringing back the jewels, we are to get a sack of gold. Ha, a fine reward!"

"Have your reward if you like," said the rabbit seizing the pixies in his strong

paws. "But let me tell you this – you're having a punishment, too, for taking our train. Why, you might never have brought it back. Six smacks each with the doll's hairbrush. Fetch it, Teddy."

Well, the pixies got their reward – but they also had their punishment, too, which was quite as it should be. They were so pleased to be rich that they gave a fine party to all the toys, and everybody went for a ride round the nursery, driven by the pixies.

They forgot the word that stopped the train, of course – but that didn't matter because all the toys knew it. They yelled it out loudly. Let me see – *what* was it? Dear me, I've forgotten. Do *you* remember?

The
Little Gold Brooch

Alison had a lovely little gold brooch with her name inside the pin. Granny had given it to her on her ninth birthday, and she was very proud of it indeed. She used it to pin her tie to her school blouse, and everyone in the school knew that the brooch had Alison's name inside.

And then one day, coming home from school, Alison lost her gold brooch. She was dreadfully upset. She was with Jenny, her friend, and Jenny could see that Alison was almost crying.

"Don't worry, Alison," she said. "We'll walk slowly back down the lane and look for your brooch. We are sure to find it."

So the two girls walked back down

the lane, looking for the little gold bar. How they hunted down that lane! Jenny even looked in the ditch, though Alison said that was silly.

"I didn't walk in the ditch, Jenny," she said. "You know I didn't. So how could the brooch be there?"

"Well, it doesn't seem to be in the lane where you *did* walk!" said Jenny.

They went on down the lane, looking closely at every rut in the road in case the brooch was there. Then Jenny looked at her watch.

"We only ought to look for two or three minutes more," she said. "We shall be very late for our dinners."

Just then they heard a little whining noise and they saw a dog coming towards them, holding up one of its back paws.

"What's the matter with that dog?" said Jenny. "It's limping."

"Well, we can't stop to help limping dogs," said Alison. "We've wasted enough time looking for my brooch as it is!"

"But, Alison, it's in pain!" said Jenny, who loved animals and hated to see them unhappy. "Look, it's coming to us for help. Do you think it's been run over?"

"Of course not!" said Alison. "Oh, Jenny, do look for my brooch and stop worrying about the dog! My brooch is much more important. I shall cry all night if I don't find it."

Jenny said no more. She looked for the brooch and the dog followed close beside her, whimpering. Then Alison heard the church clock striking a quarter past one and she cried out in dismay:

"I *shall* be late! I must go, and perhaps I'll have time to hunt again on my way back to school this afternoon. Thanks for helping me, Jenny. Come on."

"You go, Alison. I'm going to see if I can find out what's wrong with this dog and perhaps take it to its home," said Jenny. Alison gave a scornful laugh and ran off.

"I think you're silly!" she cried, and rushed home up the lane.

Jenny took the dog's head between her hands and looked into its big eyes. "What's the matter?" she said. "Shall I look at that limping leg for you? Will you let me?"

"Woof!" said the dog, and licked her hand. Jenny turned him round and lifted up the leg that seemed to be hurting the dog. It wasn't broken.

"Perhaps you have a thorn in your paw," said Jenny. "Let me look. I won't hurt you."

The dog let her look. Jenny turned the paw up so that she could see the pad underneath – and she gave a cry of astonishment.

"Good gracious! You poor thing! You have trodden on Alison's gold brooch and the pin of it has stuck into your pad! No wonder you limped! It must have hurt you dreadfully, much worse than a thorn."

"Woof!" said the dog humbly, licking Jenny's hand again.

"Now you must let me take it out," said Jenny. "I shall have to hurt you just a tiny little bit, but it will soon be over, and I am sure you are a brave dog, aren't you?"

"Woof!" said the dog happily. He liked Jenny so much that he didn't mind

what she did to him. The little girl took firm hold of the pin, gave it a sharp pull – and hey presto, it was out!

"There!" she said. "That's all right now. Look at the funny thorn you had in your paw, dog! Well, you can go home now and walk on all your four feet again!"

"Woof, woof!" said the dog, licking Jenny's bare leg, and running off in delight down the lane. He meant always to look out for that kind girl again whenever he went for a walk.

Jenny put the brooch into her bag. "If Alison had been kind and helped the dog, she would have had her brooch by

67

now," said Jenny to herself. "As it is, she will have to wait till this afternoon."

Jenny went home to dinner, and told her mother the whole story. "You did right, Jenny," said her mother. "I am glad you were kind."

Alison came to school that afternoon with red eyes. Her mother had scolded her hard for losing her brooch, and Alison now felt quite sure she would never, never find it again. Jenny ran to meet her.

"Here's your gold brooch!" she said, and she told Alison where she had found it. Alison listened and went red.

"I feel ashamed, Jenny," she said in a small voice. "My brooch would never have been found if you hadn't had a kind heart. Don't think too badly of me, Jenny. Every time I pin my brooch on to my tie I shall think how kindness got it back for me."

And she does. As for the dog, he never forgot Jenny, and now he goes for a long walk with her every Saturday and Sunday. I see them each weekend!

Simple Simon
Goes to Camp

Have you heard the story about Simple
Simon going to camp? You haven't?
Well, I must tell it to you.

Now Simple Simon had never been
away from home – but one day his
schoolteacher asked him if he would like
to go to camp with the other boys.

"It would do you good, Simon," he
said. "You're too dreamy and forgetful.
You ask your mother if she'll let you
come along with us and camp out on
Breezy Hill."

Simon ran home to ask his mother.
He was terribly excited. All the other
boys had been to camp, but not Simon.

His mother said yes, he could go, and
Simon was mad with delight. "I'll be so
helpful," he said. "I'll do everything I'm

told. I'll learn how to put up a tent and take one down. I'll do the washing-up. I'll – I'll – I'll do anything!"

Well, Simon went to camp with the other boys. He had his kit-bag on his back, full of the things he would need. It was heavy, but he didn't mind. The other boys grinned when they saw Simple Simon coming with them.

"Hello, Simple Simon," they said. "Have you met your pieman yet?"

That was an old joke, and Simon smiled. He was so excited that he didn't mind anything. He went with the others to Breezy Hill. It was a good name for it, because the wind blew there all the time.

70

Simon learnt how to put up a tent – but he didn't learn it very well, because it always fell down on top of him as soon as he got inside. He learnt how to wash dirty cups and plates in the clear little stream, but after he had fallen in twice he wasn't allowed to do that any more.

Then he was told to go and fetch the milk, and he was given a big jug. So off went Simon – but after a bit, when he got into the next field, he stood and thought.

"I didn't ask where I was to get the milk from," he said to himself. "How stupid! The boys will all laugh at me if I go back and ask. I wonder where Jimmy got the milk from yesterday?"

71

"Moo-oo-oooo!" said a nearby cow and looked so hard at Simon that he felt sure she was answering him.

"Oh, of course – milk comes from cows," said Simon. "I must milk a cow. Hi, you cow – come over here a minute, will you?"

He waved his jug at the cow, but she turned her head away and went on chewing. She was lying down, and she didn't mean to get up for Simon.

"Now look here, cow," said Simon, going up to her. "You know what this milk jug's for, don't you? Don't pretend to me that you don't know what milk is!

Just get up and fill this jug for me. Do you want to keep the boys waiting for their breakfast?"

The cow didn't mind about that at all. She whisked her tail round and hit Simon on the legs.

"Don't," said Simon. "Aren't you going to get up, cow? I'll help you."

He gave her a push, but she lay there like an elephant, quite unpushable. Simon glared at her for a minute and then heard someone calling over the hedge.

"Simon! Bring the milk quickly, we're waiting!"

Simon ran to the hedge. "The cow won't give me any. She's most obstinate."

"Idiot! You get the milk at the farm!" said the boy over the hedge. "Don't tell me you've been arguing with the cow! Here, give me the jug, and *I'll* go!"

He squeezed through the hedge, snatched the jug from poor Simon and set off to the farm. And how Simon was teased when the other boys knew he had asked the cow to fill the milk jug!

"Well, we shan't ask you to do any more jobs," they said. "Not another single one, Simon! You never use your brains, you're so slow for words." Poor Simon. He was very upset. It was quite true he didn't think hard enough. His mother was always telling him so.

Nobody asked him to help after that. Even when he offered he wasn't allowed to. It wasn't any fun to go camping and not share in the work. Poor Simon felt very unhappy.

"Please let me help," he begged Jimmy, when he saw him preparing the dinner for the boys. "Can't I peel potatoes?"

"No. Last time you did that you left half the peel on," said Jimmy. "Go away. I'm making a stew, and I want it to be good."

"What are you putting into it?" asked Simon.

"Carrots – onions – parsnips – turnips," said Jimmy. "Blow – I've not got the turnips."

74

"Let *me* get them for you!" said Simon at once.

"You don't know a turnip from a banana!" said Jimmy scornfully.

"I do, I do," said Simon. "They grow in the field over there, don't they?"

"Yes," said Jimmy, "and the farmer said we might pull what we wanted. Well – you go and bring me some, Simon. And don't you dare to come back with onions or carrots – it's *turnips* I want, see?"

Simon set off. He came back after a moment, thinking hard. "How many do you want?" he asked. "Twenty?"

75

"No, silly! Three will do nicely," said Jimmy, beginning to peel potatoes. "Now do go."

Simon went – but he was back again in half a minute. "You didn't tell me what size," he said. "Do you want big ones or small ones?"

"Big ones," said Jimmy, getting annoyed.

"How big?" asked Simon.

"Oh – just about as big as your head," said Jimmy. "Now GO, Simon, or you'll not get the turnips till teatime."

Simon went. He climbed over the stile and got into the turnip field. He looked at the turnips. They were in their

76

hundreds, the root part well in the ground, and green leaves sticking up in tufts.

"I wonder how big my head is," said Simon to himself, and he felt it to see. "How can I possibly tell if those turnips are as big as my head? I can't *see* my head, and I really don't know how big it is."

He didn't like to go back and ask what size his head was. He felt that Jimmy would be very cross if he did. And yet how cross he would be if he brought back turnips too big or too small! It was a puzzle to know what to do.

"I must use my brains," said Simple Simon to himself. "I must think hard. There must be some way of knowing which turnips are as big as my head. Now – what shall I do?"

He thought very hard indeed. Then he smiled, because he had thought of a way to solve his puzzle.

"My hat fits my head," he said, and he took it off. "Now – if only I can find three turnips that fit my hat well I shall

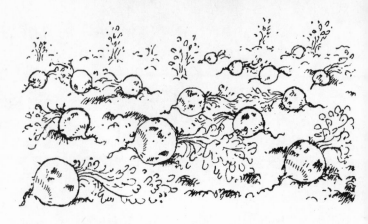

know they are the same size as my head." He pulled up a turnip. He turned it upside down and fitted his hat over it. Then he threw the turnip away.

"You're too small, turnip," he said. "My hat doesn't fit you. I'll get another." He pulled up another turnip, an enormous one, and fitted his hat over it. But it wouldn't go on!

"You're too large, turnip," he said, and threw it away. "You're bigger than my head. *You* won't do!"

He tried another, but that was too big, too. Then he found one that exactly fitted his hat. How pleased he was!

"Good turnip," he said, and he patted

it. "Very good turnip! You're the same size as my head, because my hat fits you!"

He pulled up another and another and another. But none of them fitted the hat, so he threw them away. After a long time he found two more that his hat fitted nicely. He put the three turnips under his arm, and his hat on his head, and set off back to the camp.

Jimmy was beginning to think Simon was never coming. "Gosh, what a time you've been!" he said, and Simon was disappointed that Jimmy didn't notice that the turnips were exactly the same size as his head.

Simon felt pleased with himself as he sat round the camp dinner with the others. "I fetched the turnips," he told everyone. "I really did help, and I didn't do anything silly, because I used my brains."

Now, about a minute after that a big man came striding up to the camp. It was Mr Straw, the farmer. He looked *most* annoyed.

"Afternoon, sir," he said to Simon's schoolteacher, who was camping with the boys. "I want to know who's been pulling up half my turnips and left them lying in the field."

"Good gracious – it can't be any of *my* boys," said the master, surprised. "They're all very well behaved."

"Sorry, sir – but it must be one of your boys," said the farmer. "And what I want to know is, who is it?"

"I tell you it can't be one of my boys," said the master. "They wouldn't do a thing like that – pull up turnips and let them go to waste."

Then he suddenly caught sight of Simon, who had gone as red as a beetroot. "Simon, *you* haven't done such a naughty thing, have you?" he asked sternly.

"Oh, sir, Jimmy sent me to get three turnips the size of my head," wailed Simon. "And I didn't know what size my head was, so I took off my hat and chose three turnips that fitted into it, and threw the rest away."

There was a silence, and then what a roar of laughter! It was too funny to think of Simon solemnly trying his hat on one turnip after another. Even the farmer smiled.

"Well, I suppose he meant no harm, but it was a brainless thing to do," he said; and that upset Simon very much, because he really had thought he was using his brains out in the turnip field. "I'll have to ask you to let the boy come along and pick up all the turnips, sir, and bring them to my shed."

So that was how poor Simon spent the whole of his afternoon – picking up turnips and taking them half a mile away to the shed.

And now Jimmy thinks he will send him to pull new carrots as big as his fingers – and everyone is wondering if dear old Simon will take his gloves along to see which carrots fit into the fingers. Do you think he will?

The
Poisonous Berries

"Let's go for a walk and see if the nuts are getting ripe!" said Harry. "Yes, let's," said Jane. "We'll get Anna and Jack, too, and perhaps George will come if he's done his work."

"Are you going out?" called Mother. "Well, now, be careful not to eat any berries that you don't know. You're safe with blackberries and bilberries – but no others, mind!"

"Mother does fuss over us," said Harry impatiently. "We should know by the taste if any berries weren't good for us! Hi, Anna! Hi, Jack! Coming for a walk to see if there are any nuts ripe yet?"

"Yes, rather!" cried Jack. "George! Have you finished your homework?

Come along, too."

So the five children went for a good long walk to the woods. By the time they got there they were hungry.

"Ooooh! I could eat about a hundred nuts!" said Jack. "I do hope we find some."

"There ought to be some blackberries, too," said Jane, looking all about. "But I think heaps of people must have been here before us – there's not a single berry to be seen!"

"And we couldn't find a single bilberry, either, as we came across the common," said George. "Well, let's hope there are some nuts. Oh, look! There's a big cluster up there in that hazel tree!"

But alas! Not one of the green nuts was ripe. It was too early in the autumn for them. The children were disappointed.

"I do wish we'd brought some chocolate or something with us," said Harry. "I really am hungry."

"Look! Don't those berries look gorgeous!" cried Jane, suddenly pointing

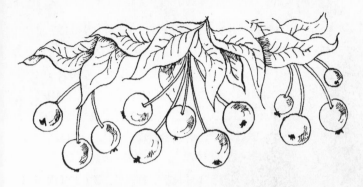

to some brilliant red berries growing on a small plant in a wet ditch. "Shall we taste them?"

"Of course not," said Anna at once. "You know what our mothers say – we must never eat strange berries."

"Well, I don't see that a taste would do any harm," said George. "I'm jolly hungry. If they taste sweet and good they'll be all right."

"Let's taste them," said Harry.

"I think you're very silly," said Anna.

"Old prim and proper!" said Jane, laughing. "You needn't have any!"

The children picked the berries and put them into their mouths. Jack spat his out at once.

"Don't like it," he said.

George rolled his round his tongue and then spat it out, too. "Not sweet enough for me," he said.

Harry tried to swallow his, choked, and spat it out. "It doesn't taste too good," he said. "Spit yours out, Jane."

But Jane wouldn't. She was always more daring than the rest. "It's nice!" she said. "Lovely and juicy! I'll have one or two more."

"You're silly," said Anna. "I shall tell your mother. You're being dangerous."

"Tell-tale-tit! Tell-tale-tit!" shouted everyone, dancing round Anna. She went very red.

"I don't care," she said. "There are times when tales have to be told – when

86

it's only sensible to tell them. Suppose Jane gets ill and nobody knows what's the matter with her? Wouldn't you all be glad if I'd told her mother and she knew how to make her better, then?"

"I shan't be ill!" said Jane, dancing about, chewing the berries. "You're an old fuss-pot!"

But, do you know, long before they got home, Jane began to feel rather ill. Her face went white and she felt sick. She didn't say a word to the others. She didn't want Anna to say, "I told you so!"

She ran indoors when she got home, and went up to her bedroom. She really felt very sick indeed. But she wasn't going to tell Mother. She just wouldn't!

But Anna did. She went into the kitchen, where Jane's mother was ironing some clothes, and spoke to her.

"Please, Mrs Brown," she said. "I don't think Jane is very well. She looked very white when she was coming home."

"Oh dear!" said Jane's mother in alarm. "What do you think is the matter with her?"

"Will you think I am telling tales if I tell you?" asked Anna.

"Of course not, if it is something to do with Jane not being well," said Mrs Brown. "It would be only sensible to tell me!"

"Well, Mrs Brown, Jane ate some bright red berries out of the ditch," said Anna. "I'm afraid they were poisonous!"

"Thank you for telling me!" cried Mrs Brown and she rushed upstairs to find Jane.

Jane was very ill. Her mother put her to bed, and called the doctor. When he had heard that she had eaten poisonous berries he was worried. He gave her a very nasty drink that made her sick.

"Maybe that will get rid of the poison," he said. Jane ached and cried, and didn't want anything to eat at all for two days.

The other children were frightened. "We ought to have taken Anna's advice," they said. "We called her an old fuss-pot – but she was right."

"And my mother says that if she hadn't been sensible enough to go and tell Mrs Brown at once that Jane had eaten strange berries, Jane might have been much worse than she was," said George. "But Mrs Brown was able to call in the doctor at once."

"Well, there's one thing I've made up *my* mind about!" said Jack. "And that is – I shall never eat any berries I don't know in future!"

Jane got better in four days. She still looked rather white when she came downstairs. She was pleased to see Anna when she called with some barley-sugar for her.

"Anna," said Jane, "I'm *so* glad you told tales about me to my mother! You were the only sensible one of the lot!"

"Well, don't eat poisonous berries any more, or I'll have to tell tales of you again!" laughed Anna.

You won't either, will you? And if there are any of your friends who are silly about berries, just lend them this story. They'll be careful after that!

The Two
Bad Brownies

Once there were two bad brownies called Click and Snip. They were bad because they took things that didn't belong to them. Once, in the summertime, they had taken some sweets from Dame Sleepy's stall in the market – and she had seen them, although they thought she was fast asleep!

And, my goodness me, what a scolding she gave them! She took hold of their skinny arms, shook them hard, and then sent them packing.

"Next time you are caught taking what doesn't belong to you, I will see that you are smacked and sent to work for the Busy-Brownie!" she called.

That frightened Click and Snip. The

Busy-Brownie worked all day long and sometimes all night too, and both Click and Snip were far too lazy to enjoy working like that. So for quite a long time they were good.

And then, when the cold days of March came, and their larder was empty, they longed for carrot soup. But they had no carrots, and no money to buy any. So what were they to do?

"There are plenty of carrots in Old Man Whiskers' field," said Click, looking at Snip.

"I know," said Snip. "But Old Man

Whiskers has a very hard hand. Suppose he caught us?"

"He goes to sleep every afternoon," said Click. "I know, because I've often heard him snoring."

"Well – if he sleeps, perhaps we could go and dig up a few carrots for soup," said Snip. "But wait a minute, Click – Crawler the Toad lives under a stone at the edge of the field."

"Pooh, what does that matter? You know he has been asleep for weeks and weeks," said Click.

"Well, what about Curl-Up the Hedgehog?" said Snip. "He has a hole in the bank near Whiskers' field. He might see us."

"Not he!" said Click. "He has been asleep for weeks too, and hasn't even stirred, not even when I stuck a twig into his hole and poked him."

"That's true," said Snip. "But wait – Slide-Along the Snake lives under the wood-pile in Old Man Whiskers' yard, and that looks on to the field. Supposing *he* saw us? *He* might tell."

"Snip, Slide-Along hasn't been awake since the autumn," said Click. "He has been curled up all through the cold weather. He won't see us!"

"Well, what about Dimmy the Dormouse?" asked Snip. "His sharp eyes take in everything, and you know where *he* lives – just under the roots of the old oak tree by the carrot-field. He would tell tales of us for sure if he saw us."

"He's fast asleep too," said Click. "I went to peep at him two weeks ago, and he didn't even move a whisker!"

"All right," said Snip. "We'll go this afternoon. I'll carry a sack and you can take a spade."

So the two bad brownies went along to Whiskers' field that afternoon. They could hear the old man snoring away in his little cottage. They set to work to dig up carrots for their soup, first looking round to make sure that no one was about.

Crawler the Toad was under his stone – but he wasn't asleep! The fingers of the March sun had crept into his damp hiding-place and warmed him. He had woken up! He heard the two bad brownies, and peeped out at them with his beautiful coppery eyes. How he frowned when he saw what they were doing.

Curl-Up the Hedgehog was awake too. The sun had brought him out of his winter sleep. He peeped out from his hole and saw Click and Snip.

Slide-Along the Snake was stretching out his long, slippery body in the wood-pile. He could not sleep any longer, because spring was coming, when all things wake. He heard the sound of the spade digging, and saw the two bad brownies working away in the field, stealing Whiskers' carrots.

And even little Dimmy, the sleepy dormouse, was awake that sunny March afternoon. He had slept tight all the winter – but now it was spring, and he was hungry. He peeped out from his hole, and watched Click and Snip.

"My, what a shock Old Man Whiskers will get when he finds half his carrots gone!" said naughty Click, with a giggle. Crawler, Curl-Up, Slide-Along, and Dimmy heard him. They all listened and frowned. They watched the two bad brownies tie up the neck of the sack and go home.

Then, after a while, they saw Old Man Whiskers come out, yawning – and

how he stared when he saw that a whole row of his precious carrots was gone!

"Now who has been along here?" he cried, in a rage.

"Click and Snip, the two bad brownies!" called Crawler, Curl-Up, Slide-Along, and Dimmy. "We saw them – we saw them!"

Old Man Whiskers took a stick and went to the little cottage where Click and Snip lived. He marched up to the door, banged on it and opened it. And there, inside, were the two brownies, cutting up carrots for soup!

"Ooooh!" said Click, in fright. Whiskers caught hold of them both. Whack, whack! My goodness, what a

97

shock for the two bad brownies! They rushed all round the kitchen trying to get away from the cross old man, but they couldn't.

"That will teach you to take my carrots!" said Whiskers, when at last his stick had broken in half. "And now, off you go to the Busy-Brownie. You know quite well that people who are too lazy to work honestly for their food have to be sent to someone who will keep them busy all day long! Off you go!"

And off they went. The Busy-Brownie was glad to see them, for he had so much work to do that he was simply longing for help. He set the two bad brownies to do hundreds of jobs, and, my goodness me, they had never worked so hard in all their lives. It was very good for them too.

Crawler the Toad, Curl-Up the Hedgehog, Slide-Along the Snake, and Dimmy the Dormouse came to watch them hurrying about their endless jobs.

"We told Old Man Whiskers about you," they said. "Bad little brownies! We told Old Man Whiskers about you!"

"But how could you do that?" cried Click. "You sleep all the winter through! You couldn't have seen us!"

"Ah, but it's spring now, and we wake up then! Didn't you know that?" said Dimmy. "We're all wide awake now – and we saw you, we saw you!"

"How stupid we were!" said Snip. "We forgot you woke up in the spring!"

Did you know they all woke up then? Well, they do!

99

At the
Bus Stop

Quite a lot of people were standing at the bus stop. David and Sara were there, of course, because they always caught the bus back home from school at that time. John, a boy in their class, was there too, and Rachel, who was in the class above.

There were two men and two women as well, talking together. "The bus is late," said one. "I wish it would hurry up. I want to get home."

David and Sara wanted to get home, too. It was exams the next day and they wanted to read their notes over and over so that they would do good geography and history papers. Bother the bus!

There suddenly came a little tinkling noise, and one of the women gave a cry.

"Oh! My bracelet has slipped off my wrist! Where is it?"

Everyone looked down to see. But it wasn't there. The woman pointed to a drain just beside the kerb. "It went down there. Look – you can just see it between the bars of the grating! Can one of you lift up the grating and get it for me?"

But nobody could. It seemed to be fastened down so that it couldn't be lifted. The woman bent down and tried to slip her hand through the grating.

"My hand's too big," she said. "I

wonder – would one of these children have a small enough hand to slip through and get my bracelet? It's such a valuable one."

"The bus is coming," said John, "I can't stop to try. Come on, Rachel. You'll miss the bus if you try to get the bracelet."

John, Rachel and one of the men and the other woman all got on the bus. It rumbled off, leaving Sara, David, the woman who had lost her bracelet and the man who was with her. The woman was almost crying now.

"It was the lovely bracelet you gave me when you married me," she said to the man. "Oh, *can't* we get it?"

David had stayed behind to see if he could manage to get the bracelet for the woman. It was a nuisance to miss the bus but, after all, you had to help if you could.

"I'll try," he said, and knelt down. But his hand was *just* too big.

"*I'll* try," said Sara, though she hated the idea of putting her hand down into the dirty, smelly drain. Oooh, how horrid!

But her small hand slid through easily and her fingers groped for the bracelet. They touched it. She got it between her two longest fingers, and carefully edged her hand back through the grating. David bent over and caught the bracelet

as soon as it appeared above the grating. He held it up to the delighted woman.

"Oh, *thank* you! That's marvellous! What's your name? I must give you a reward."

"No, that's all right," said David and Sara together, and they ran off down the road, because they knew that they could get home before the next bus came – there was such a long wait in between the buses in the late afternoon.

The two children felt pleased when they got home. It was nice to know they had got back the bracelet. Mother was pleased about it, too.

But when David got out his notes to

revise them after tea he didn't feel at all pleased. He had lost his precious fountain-pen!

He felt in all his pockets. Then he smacked his hand crossly on the table. "Sara! It must have slipped out when I was kneeling down over that grating! I *thought* I felt something sliding by my knee, but I was so taken up with the bracelet I didn't look to see."

"Oh, David! We got the bracelet, but we lost your pen! And it's exams tomorrow!" said Sara. "We didn't deserve to lose your pen. I'd lend you mine for the exams, but the nib has gone all crooked and it's simply dreadful to write with now. Oh dear – now you'll have to use an ordinary biro. That *will* put you off your exams!"

"We'll look for the pen when we get off the bus tomorrow," said David gloomily. "But someone will be sure to have seen it and picked it up."

It wasn't there, of course. David went to school feeling very mournful – his nice pen lost – and just as exams were on, too – and Sara's pen wasn't much use, either. It wasn't any good borrowing that.

After prayers that morning, just as the children turned to march out, the headmaster held up his hand.

"One moment," he said. "I have a letter here. It concerns two children from this school who missed the bus yesterday through doing someone a kindness – getting a valuable bracelet from a drain. They wouldn't give their names or take a reward. Who were those two children, please?"

David and Sara stood out, blushing fiery red. Good gracious! Fancy anyone writing a letter about them!

The headmaster smiled at them. "Thank you for bringing credit to the school," he said. "With the letter was a parcel for you. Here it is."

David took it, and when he opened it – guess what was inside! Yes, you're right – two smart fountain-pens, one for him and one for Sara! What a bit of luck!

"*I expect you've both got fine fountain-pens,*" said the note with the presents. "*But you never know when they might get broken or be lost – so here are two, just in case!*"

You should have seen the children's faces!

"It's like magic!" said Sara, beaming. "*Now* we shall be able to write some fine exam papers!"

They did, of course – and they were top. Their mother was very pleased, indeed – and so am I. It's just the sort of thing that *should* happen, isn't it?

The
Christmas Tree
Aeroplane

All the children in the village were as excited as could be, because the lady at the Big House was giving a party – and every boy and girl was invited!

"I'm going to wear my new suit!" said Alan.

"I'm going to have on my new blue dress," said Lucy.

"There are going to be crackers and balloons!" said John.

"And an ENORMOUS Christmas tree that nearly reaches the ceiling!" said Harry.

"And a lovely tea with jellies and chocolate cake!" said Belinda.

"It will be the loveliest party that ever was!" said Michael.

"Look! There's the tree going up to

the Big House!" cried Freddie. All the children ran into the lane and watched the cart going up the snowy road, with a big Christmas tree lying on it.

"There's a fine pack of toys for this tree!" called the driver, who was Alan's father. "I've seen them. My, you'll be lucky children!"

"What's for the top of the tree?" asked Belinda. "Will there be a fairy doll?"

"No, not this year," said the driver. "There is something different – it's Santa Claus in an aeroplane! He's going to be at the top of the tree, looking

109

mighty grand in his plane, I can tell you!"

"How lovely!" cried all the children – and they thought that it would be even nicer to have Santa Claus in an aeroplane at the top of the Christmas tree than a fairy doll.

At last the great day came. Everybody was dressed in their best. Every girl wore new ribbons and every boy had brushed his hair down flat till it shone. They all went up to the Big House as happy as could be.

At least, all of them except Harry. He went with the others, but he didn't feel very happy. His suit wasn't new – it was only his old one, because he hadn't a best one. His shoes wanted mending, and he hadn't even got a clean hanky, because his mother was ill in bed and couldn't see to him properly. But Harry had washed his face and hands, and brushed his hair as well as he possibly could.

He soon forgot about his old suit and his old shoes. The children shouted with joy when they went into the big hall and saw the Christmas tree there. Its candles were not yet lighted, but all the ornaments and presents hung on it, and it looked beautiful.

"Look! There's the aeroplane at the top of the tree!" cried Michael. Everyone looked – and, dear me, it certainly was a

very fine aeroplane. It shone and glittered, and the little Santa Claus inside grinned in a jolly way at all the children.

"I wonder who will have the aeroplane for a present," said John.

Mrs Lee, the lady who was giving the party, smiled at him. "Nobody will have the aeroplane," she said. "I bought it to go at the top of the tree, not for a present. It is just to make the tree look pretty."

The party was lovely. There were games of all kinds and there were prizes for those who won the games. Everybody won one except Harry, who really was very unlucky.

Then balloons were given out. Harry got a great big blue one. He was very proud of it. And just as he was throwing it up into the air, playing with it, he heard someone's balloon go pop!

It was little Janey's. She had thrown it by mistake against a spray of prickly holly, and it had burst. Janey burst too – into tears! She sobbed and sobbed – but

there was not another balloon left for her to have.

Harry went up to her. "Have my balloon, Janey," he said. "Here it is. It's a beauty. You have it, and then you won't cry any more."

Janey was simply delighted. She took the blue balloon and smiled through her tears. "Oh, thank you, Harry," she said. "I do love it!"

Wasn't it nice of Harry? He watched Janey playing with his balloon until teatime – and then the children sat down to a lovely tea. Oh, the cakes there were, and the dishes of jellies and blancmanges! They really did enjoy themselves.

At the end of tea, Mrs Lee gave each child three crackers. They pulled them with a loud pop-pop-pop. Out came toys and hats.

Harry was unlucky with his crackers. The other children who pulled with him got the toys out of his crackers – and he only got a hat. And *that* was a bonnet, so he gave it to Ruth.

The next exciting thing that happened was the Christmas tree! All the children went into the hall, and there was the tree lighted up from top to bottom with

114

pink, yellow, blue, green, and red candles. It looked like a magic tree.

"Isn't it lovely!" cried all the children. "Oh, isn't it lovely!"

Then Mrs Lee began to cut the presents off. As she did so, she called out a child's name.

"Michael!" And up went Michael and took a train.

"Belinda!" And up went Belinda and was handed a beautiful doll.

"Alan!" Up went Alan and had a big fat book of stories. It was so exciting.

115

But one little boy was left out! It wasn't Harry – he had a ship. It was Paul. For some reason he had been forgotten, and there was no present for him at all. Mrs Lee smiled at all the children and told them to go into the dining-room again to play some more games – and Paul didn't like to say he had had no present from the tree.

"Where's your present, Paul?" asked Harry, as they went into the big dining-room.

"I didn't get one," said Paul, trying to look as if he didn't mind. "Perhaps Mrs Lee doesn't like me. I was rather naughty last week, and she may have heard of it."

"But, Paul, aren't you unhappy because you haven't got anything?" said Harry who thought Paul was being very brave about it.

"Yes," said Paul, and he turned away so that Harry shouldn't see how near to crying he was. It was so dreadful to be left out like that.

Harry thought it was dreadful too. He put his arm round Paul. "Take my ship," he said. "I've got one at home. I don't need this, Paul."

Paul turned round, his face shining. "Have you really got a ship at home, Harry?" he said. "Are you sure you don't want it?"

Harry *did* want it – but he saw that Paul wanted it badly too. So the kind-hearted boy pushed his precious ship into Paul's hands, and then went to join in a game.

When half-past six came, the party

was over. Mothers and fathers had come to fetch their children. How they cried out in surprise when they saw the balloons, the cracker-toys, and the lovely presents and prizes that their children had.

Only Harry had none. His mother did not come to fetch him because she was ill. His father was looking after her, so Harry had to walk the long dark way home by himself. It was snowing, and the little boy turned up his collar.

He went to say goodbye and thank you to Mrs Lee. He had good manners, and he knew that at the end of a party or a treat every child should say thank you very much.

"Goodbye, Mrs Lee, and thank you very much for asking me to your nice

118

party," said Harry politely.

"I'm glad you enjoyed it," said Mrs Lee, shaking hands with him. "But wait a minute – you have forgotten your things. Where is your balloon? And your cracker-toys – and your present? You surely don't want to leave them behind."

Harry went red. He didn't know what to say. But little Janey called out loudly:

"Oh, Mrs Lee, my balloon burst, so Harry gave me his lovely blue one. Here it is!"

"And he only got a bonnet out of one of his crackers, and he couldn't wear it because he is a boy," said Ruth, holding up the red bonnet. "So he gave it to me."

"But where is your present?" asked Mrs Lee. "I know I gave you a ship!"

"Here's the ship!" said Paul, holding it up. "He gave it to me."

"But why did you do that, Harry?" asked Mrs Lee in surprise. "Didn't you like it?"

"I loved it," said Harry, going redder

and redder. "But you see, Mrs Lee, Paul
didn't get a present. You forgot him.
And he really was very brave about it,
so I gave him the ship."

"Well!" said Mrs Lee in astonishment.
"I think you must be the most generous
boy I've ever known. But I can't let you
go away from my party without
something! Wait a minute and let me
see if there is anything left."

She looked in the balloon box. No
balloons. She looked into the cracker
boxes. No crackers! She looked on the
tree – not a present was left! Only the
ornaments were there, shining and
glittering.

"Dear me, there doesn't seem to be
anything left at all," said Mrs Lee. And
then she caught sight of the beautiful
shining aeroplane at the top, with Santa
Claus smiling inside. "Of course!
There's that! I didn't mean anyone to
have it, because it is such a beauty and I
wanted it for the next time we had the
tree – but you shall have it, Harry,
because you deserve it!"

And she got a chair, cut down the lovely aeroplane, and gave it to Harry. He was so excited that he could hardly say thank you. He had got the loveliest thing of all!

The other children crowded round him to see. "Ooooh! Isn't it lovely!" they said. "How it shines! And isn't Santa Claus real? You *are* lucky, Harry – but you deserve it."

"Yes, he deserves it," said Mrs Lee, smiling. "And I am going to take him home in my car, because I don't want him to be lost in the snow. Wait for me, Harry!"

So Harry waited, hugging his fine aeroplane, and feeling happier than he had ever been in his life. And when Mrs Lee came up with her coat on, she carried a box of cakes and a big dish of fruit jelly for Harry's mother.

"I thought I was going home with nothing – and I'm going home with more than anybody else," said Harry in delight.

"A kind heart always brings its own reward," said Mrs Lee. "Remember that, Harry!"

He always does remember it – and we will too, won't we?

Mrs Muddle's Scarf

"I've got to catch a train this morning," said Mrs Muddle to her Aunt Brinnie. "I'm going to have lunch with a dear old friend of mine, who's back from America. She says she's got a fine present to give me. Isn't that nice?"

"Very nice," said Aunt Brinnie, looking round at the muddle of unwashed breakfast things, the unswept floor and the undusted room. "Well, you'll have to hurry up, Mary Muddle, and get your house clean, if you're going to catch the twelve o'clock train!"

"Mandy! Mandy!" called Mrs Muddle to her daily help. "Come and clear away. We'll have to look sharp this morning because I've got to catch a train."

Mandy hurried in. Aunt Brinnie put

on a coat to go and feed the hens. "I should think you'd better sweep this floor, Mary Muddle," she said. "It's in a dreadful state – crumbs and bits of fluff all over the place. Somebody might call this afternoon and I should feel very ashamed of it."

"All right, all right," said Mrs Muddle and fetched a broom. But such a cloud of dust arose from the dirty carpet that she began to cough. "I'd better tie up my hair," she said. "I washed it last night, and if I don't put something round my head it'll be all dirty again."

So she fetched a scarf and tied it round her head. Then she began to sweep again. How she swept! Aunt Brinnie put her head in at the door once and took it out again. It would be at least an hour before the dust settled, she thought.

Mrs Muddle felt cross. What a nuisance Aunt Brinnie was, always telling her to do this and that. She would tell Mandy she could go out, and she wouldn't leave anything for Aunt

Brinnie's lunch except a bit of dry cheese. If Aunt Brinnie wanted anything else she could cook it for herself.

When she had swept and dusted, Mrs Muddle looked at the clock. Good gracious! She would hardly have time to get herself ready and make herself look really nice before the train went!

She untied her apron and threw it over a chair. She hurried upstairs and began to pull out her things. Bother, bother, bother, there was a ladder in her best stockings, and now she would have

to mend it, just when she had hardly any time!

She mended it. Then she looked for her best shoes. They had a button off. Oh, dear – of course, she remembered now, it had come off last week, and she had forgotten to put it on again. Could anything be more annoying?

By the time she had put on a button another ten minutes had gone by. Mrs Muddle began to dress in a hurry, not even bothering to look at herself in the glass.

"My best dress – my little black coat – my necklace – my black bag. Oh dear, oh dear, there's a spot down the front of my dress, and it just shows in the opening of my coat!"

She looked down at the spot in dismay. She really couldn't go out to lunch with a dirty spot on her dress, just in front, too! But there was no time to clean it.

"I'll wear my scarf!" thought Mrs Muddle. "That will hide the dirty spot nicely."

She found her hat-box, took out her big hat and crammed it on her head. Now where was her scarf?

She opened the top drawer. No scarf. It wasn't in the next one either. Mrs Muddle grew anxious, and pulled out everything in the drawer, scattering gloves, hankies and stockings all over the floor.

She looked in the wardrobe. She looked on her dressing-table. No scarf there. Where could it be? Oh dear, oh

dear, the time was going, and still she hadn't found that scarf.

"Mary Muddle, you'll lose your train if you don't hurry!" called Aunt Brinnie.

"Aunt Brinnie, what have I done with my scarf?" called Mrs Muddle. "I know I had it yesterday."

"Yes, you lent it to the little boy who came to tea," said Aunt Brinnie. "He wanted to be a train-guard and wave a flag, and you lent it to him for that."

"So I did, so I did," said Mrs Muddle, hurrying down the stairs. "I put it away with the clockwork train and the rails. That's what I did." But it wasn't there. Mandy came running in. "Mrs Muddle, don't you remember, you told me you wanted to shade one of the lamps yesterday evening, because it was too bright, and you fetched your scarf from the toy cupboard and draped it over the lamp?"

"I know, I know!" cried Mrs Muddle, remembering. "Miss Brown came in last night and wanted to show me a new way of bandaging a broken arm, and we took the scarf off the lamp and used it for a bandage."

"Yes, and you said that when you saw Miss Brown off at the front gate it was raining, so you took the scarf and flung it over your hair," said Mandy. "What did you do with it when you came in?"

"Oh, there was a strange cat in the kitchen and I used the scarf to flap at it, to scare it out," said Mrs Muddle. "I seem to have used it for a lot of things, don't I, Mandy?"

"And after that, you probably put it into the corner over there by the brooms, to be washed," said Mandy. "It was so dirty by then!"

"Dear me, so I did," said Mrs Muddle. "I remember putting it over the broom-handle. Have you used a broom this morning, Mandy?"

"Mandy hasn't, but *you* have," said Aunt Brinnie. "You've been making a rare old dust in here all the morning with your broom. You must have seen the scarf when you took up the broom – and if you think hard, Mary Muddle, you will no doubt remember exactly what you did with it!"

Mary Muddle thought hard. Then she smacked her hand down on the table. "Of course!" she cried. "I was making such a dust that I tied the scarf round my head to keep my hair clean!"

She put her hand up to her head – but she was wearing her big hat now. Auntie Brinnie looked at her closely and began to laugh.

"Mary Muddle, you are the biggest muddler and the greatest silly I have ever met!" she said. "Do you know what you've done? You've crammed that big hat on your head without taking off

your scarf! For shame, not even to brush out your hair before you go out to lunch!"

Mary Muddle blushed bright red. She took off her hat – and, sure enough, underneath it, tied tightly round her hair, was the missing scarf!

"How silly of me," said Mary Muddle. She dragged it off and knotted it round her neck. Then she pulled on her hat again, took up her bag and ran off to the station without even saying goodbye!

"She's a real muddler, and she's got no manners at all," said Aunt Brinnie to herself, shaking her head.

131

Mandy popped her head in. "Mrs Muddle said I could go early, Miss Brinnie," she said. "I'm going now. I'm afraid there's not much for your lunch, though."

Off she went. Aunt Brinnie went to the larder and looked there. How mean of Mary! She had left just a tiny bit of stale cheese for her Aunt Brinnie, and nothing else at all unless the old lady went to the trouble of cooking herself some meat. Well, well, well – that was just like Mary Muddle!

"I shall take the bus and go out to lunch," thought old Aunt Brinnie. "I won't stay in and have that stale bit of cheese!"

So out she went and just managed to catch the bus that went to the next town. She wondered if Mary Muddle had caught her train.

She hadn't. It had gone five minutes before she reached the station, hot and bothered and untidy! So, as there was not another train till the afternoon, Mrs Muddle had to walk all the way back home, tired and disappointed.

And when she got there she called for Mandy. But Mandy had gone. "Of course – I told her to go!" thought Mrs Muddle. "Aunt Brinnie! Where are you?"

But Aunt Brinnie had gone out too. Mrs Muddle went to the larder, feeling hungry. Oh dear, oh dear, there was only that bit of stale cheese and the Sunday joint! Why had she been so mean to Aunt Brinnie? She could easily have sent Mandy out to buy some chops for

133

her. Now the shops would be shut for lunch, and there was nothing at all to eat except a tiny bit of hard cheese!

And that was all that Mary Muddle had for her dinner. She felt very sorry for herself. Then she began to be ashamed.

"If I hadn't got my work into such a muddle this week, so that I had to do all that sweeping this morning – if I hadn't forgotten to mend that ladder in my stocking – and put the button on my shoe – and wash that dirty place on my dress – if I hadn't forgotten where my scarf was – I'd have been lunching at the Grand Hotel in the next town now," she thought. "And if I hadn't been mean to Aunt Brinnie and left her only this bit of stale cheese for lunch I'd have had something nice myself when I missed my train and came back. I'm a selfish muddler!"

She had the house to herself. Mandy wouldn't be back, and goodness knows when Aunt Brinnie would return. Mrs Muddle suddenly made up her mind.

"I'm going to clean the house from top to bottom! I'm going to clean out the hen-house too! I'm going to do all the washing that's waiting to be done! I'm going to do all the mending as well!"

And away she went like a whirlwind to begin all the jobs. How she could work when she wanted to! How she cleaned and scrubbed and polished, washed and mended! How surprised the hens were to have their house cleaned out so thoroughly.

Mrs Muddle was very tired indeed by the time it was dark. She took off her dirty things, washed, tidied her hair and put on a clean dress. Then she sat down, hungry – but there was now nothing but bread and butter to eat! She had forgotten to go and buy anything at the shops.

Presently the door opened and in came Aunt Brinnie. She stopped in astonishment when she saw the bright clean room.

"Gracious!" she said. "What's happened?"

"I missed the train," said Mary Muddle. "And when I came back to an empty house I suddenly felt ashamed of myself. So I've cleaned it well. And I'm

going to try and do better now, Aunt Brinnie. I'm sorry, too, about leaving you no lunch!"

"Oh, don't worry about that!" said Aunt Brinnie. "I caught the bus and went to the next town. I thought I might get lunch at the Grand Hotel there, where you were going to meet your friend – and, dear me, there she was, still waiting for you, though you were half an hour late already. When you didn't come, she asked *me* to lunch with her instead, so I did – and, my word, we did have a fine lunch!"

"Don't, don't!" cried poor Mary Muddle, with tears in her eyes. "To think what I've missed! And I'm so dreadfully hungry now and there's still nothing in the larder except the Sunday joint!"

"Well, I've brought some eggs and bacon and some fine mushrooms," said Aunt Brinnie. "We'll have a wonderful supper. And in that parcel you'll find the present that your friend wanted to give you."

"Oh, how lovely!" cried Mrs Muddle. She opened it – and inside was another scarf, a blue one with little dark lines patterning it.

"I don't deserve it!" she cried. "Aunt Brinnie, isn't it nice!"

"Beautiful!" said her aunt, taking down the frying-pan to cook the supper. "But don't you go using it for guards' flags, or bandages, or flapping at cats!"

"Oh, I won't, I won't!" cried Mrs Muddle. She took the frying-pan from her aunt's hand. "Now you sit down and let me do this! I've been selfish to you today – but I'm different tonight!"

So Mary Muddle had her present after all, and a very nice supper, too. But Aunt Brinnie wouldn't have given her either if she hadn't come back to a clean house and a nicer Mary Muddle. You can't expect things if you don't do something for them, can you?

The Good Luck Morning

The Good Luck Morning began quite suddenly. It happened when Toppy was coming back from taking a message for his aunt. He was skipping along merrily, and was just bending down to take a stone out of his shoe, when he saw a book lying on the ground.

He forgot about the stone in his shoe and picked up the book. Inside was written, "This book belongs to Dame Spillikins."

"I'll take it over to her," said Toppy, and went off to her cottage. "She must have dropped it."

Dame Spillikins was simply delighted to have her book back. "Why, it's my book of spells, Toppy!" she said. "You're sure you haven't peeped inside and read

139

some of them?"

"No, Ma'am, of course not," said Toppy.

"I've just baked some meat pies," said Dame Spillikins, turning to her oven. "You sit down for a minute, Toppy, and I'll give you one for your kindness." Toppy sat down, beaming. "I'm in luck!" he said to the old lady. "I really am."

He ate the warm meat pie, and finished every crumb. "Most delicious!" he said to Dame Spillikins. "Thank you very much. Now I must be getting along."

So off he went. Before very long he saw little Mother Fly-Around. She had a magic broomstick that was the envy of everyone in the town. She didn't bother about buses or trains – she just sat on her broomstick, told it where to go, and it went.

Toppy had always longed for a ride on the wonderful broomstick, but he had never had one. He watched little Mother Fly-Around land in her garden and get off the broomstick – and then he saw

that she had dropped her shopping-basket, and everything had rolled out.

He ran in at the gate at once. "I'll pick them up for you, Mother Fly-Around. Don't you worry!"

And in a second, he had picked everything up and popped it back into her basket. Mother Fly-Around was pleased.

"You're a nice, good-mannered little creature," she said to Toppy. "Would you like a little ride on my broomstick?"

Well! Toppy could hardly believe his ears. Why, Mother Fly-Around *never* lent her broomstick to anyone. What a bit of luck!

141

"Oh, yes, *please*," said Toppy, thrilled, and he got on it, riding it astride like a horse. "Take me to the market and back!" he ordered, and at once the stick rose into the air and made off to the market. It was the loveliest feeling Toppy had ever had in his life, riding a broomstick!

"This is certainly my Good Luck Morning," he thought. "Hey, broomstick, you're going a bit too fast. Whooooosh!"

Down he went again to Mother Fly-Around's. "Thank you very much," he said. "I did enjoy that."

142

Off he went again, on his way back to his aunt's. Soon he met Twinkles carrying a large box of chocolates.

"Hallo, Toppy," said Twinkles. "Look what my uncle has given me! Take three!"

"Oooooh!" said Toppy, as Twinkles took off the lid and showed rows of enormous chocolates.

"*Thank* you. More good luck. I don't know what's the matter with me this morning, but I keep on and on having good luck."

"Well, you must have got something lucky on you," said Twinkles, looking at him closely. "Have you got a lucky feather in your hat? No. Have you got a lucky button on? No. Well *I* don't know what's making you lucky then. Did you pick a four-leaved clover today?"

"No," said Toppy. "I've never found

143

one in my life, though I've always wanted to. I simply can't imagine why I'm lucky today."

He went skipping on his way, and then felt the stone in his shoe again.

"I really must take it out," he thought, and bent down to take off his shoe. And there on the ground, just under his nose, was a little pearl necklace!

"Look at that now!" said Toppy, in amazement, forgetting all about taking off his shoe. "A pearl necklace! Whatever next! I must take it along to the police-station and see if anyone has lost it."

Soon he was showing it to Mr Plod, the policeman.

"My word! Where did you find it?" said Mr Plod. "It belongs to Lady Silver-Toes. There is a reward of five gold pieces offered to the finder. Here you are, Toppy. Go and spend them."

"Well, would you believe it!" said Toppy, in astonishment. "Five gold pieces – all for picking up a necklace I saw under my nose! There's no end to my luck this morning!"

Off he went, eager to get back to his aunt and tell her all about this Good Luck Morning. She was in the garden, weeding. She waved to him as he came in. "Toppy! I've left some hot ginger cakes on the table for you – and the postman has brought a parcel. It's from your grandmother, so it's sure to be something nice."

"Well, well – what good luck is following me!" thought Toppy, pleased. He popped a ginger cake into his mouth, and cut the string round the parcel.

Out came a box, and in the box was just what Toppy had longed for for weeks. It was a magic top which, once it was set spinning, would go on without stopping, and would hum a little song all the time. Some of the pixies already had them and Toppy had longed and longed for one.

"Look! A magic top!" he cried, running out to his aunt.

"Lucky boy!" she said.

"But you wait till you hear all that has happened to me this morning," said Toppy. "Look, Aunt – look at all these gold pieces. I've had nothing but good luck all the morning."

His aunt listened whilst he told her everything.

"It's most peculiar," she said. "There's *something* you've got on you somewhere, Toppy, that is bringing you this good luck. Whatever can it be?"

But Toppy couldn't think *what* it was. He looked up and down himself, but he was just the same as usual. It was most extraordinary.

"I'll just go and put these gold pieces into my money-box," he said, and he turned to go indoors. Then he felt the stone in his shoe again, and stopped.

"Bother! I've never taken that silly stone out – I've not had a minute to think about it! It's the only bit of bad luck I've had today."

147

He took off his shoe. Inside was a sharp little stone, roughly in the shape of a star, and a very bright blue in colour. Toppy picked it out of his shoe and threw it high in the air. It fell in the road somewhere.

"What was that?" asked his aunt.

"A stone out of my shoe," said Toppy, putting his shoe on again. "It's been bothering me all morning. Now, Aunt, I'm going to look out for some more good luck!"

"Well, Toppy – I'm afraid you won't get it," said his aunt. "I know what has brought you all your good luck this morning – that little blue stone in your shoe! It was a good luck stone."

Toppy stared at her in dismay. "Was it? Are you sure? Oh my, oh my, I've thrown it away into the road. Goodness knows where it's gone. Oh, Aunt – I've thrown my good luck away!"

"What a thing to do!" said his aunt. "Go and look for it before anyone else finds it, silly."

But Toppy couldn't find that tiny stone though he spent hours looking in the road. Wasn't it a pity? It's somewhere about still, I expect, so if you get a stone in your shoe, do have a look at it before you shake it away. You might have a Good Luck Morning, too, if you can get it!

Two Children
Came By

Paul was going down the road when he suddenly saw something funny in the house at the corner. He stopped. What could it be? It was a strange glow that came and went in an upper window. Then he heard a crackling noise and saw a little puff of smoke coming out of the window. He stood and stared. It was night-time, and the glow could clearly be seen, red and ugly.

Fire! Fire!

Paul knew the room was on fire. He was a timid little boy and he stood and trembled. He didn't know what to do. He couldn't make up his mind, and he was very frightened.

So what *did* he do when he saw a room on fire in the house at the corner?

He did what he always did when he was frightened. He ran away. Yes, he ran away as fast as ever he could, away from the crackling noise, away from the smoke and the glow. He ran home, panting.

"What's the matter, Paul, darling?" said his mother. "You look pale. Are you ill? What has frightened you?"

Paul didn't tell her what had scared him, and he didn't say a word about the fire. He went to bed without telling anyone. But in the middle of the night he woke up, afraid.

That fire! He hadn't told anyone. The whole room might have burnt out. The fire might have spread down the stairs.

151

There might have been little children upstairs. The people might have lost all their furniture. The fire would spread to the house next door – that might be burnt too – the whole row might be burnt. Perhaps the town would catch fire, and his house, his own house, would be burnt as well.

Paul yelled. He yelled and he yelled. His mother came running. "Paul! Paul, darling, what's the matter?"

And then he told her. She comforted him and told him not to worry. She hadn't heard of any fire. She took him to the window and showed him the quiet dark night without a gleam or glow anywhere except for the lamp that stood shining in the street.

She didn't say he should have warned someone about the fire. She didn't even say he shouldn't have run away.

He went to sleep at last, and dreamt of fires all night long.

But he needn't have worried. There was another child about that night, a boy called Jack. He came round the

corner at the same moment that Paul was rushing away down the street. And, like Paul, he saw the red glow in the window, and heard the crackling noise.

Did he run away? No, of course not. He gave a tremendous shout: "FIRE! FIRE!"

He ran to the house and pushed at the door. It was only on the latch and it opened. He rushed inside, shouting loudly. Nobody seemed to be about. The house owners were out in the garden at the back, enjoying the quiet summer night.

Jack raced up the stairs. He came to the room where the fire was. He opened the door cautiously.

He peeped in. A coal had fallen out on the rug. The rug had caught fire and had burnt the waste-paper basket. The

basket stood near the curtains that blew in the wind at the open window. They were blazing too.

In a cot lay a little girl, asleep. She looked only about two years old. Her big teddy-bear sat beside her, looking at Jack out of big glass eyes.

Jack knew what to do. He picked up the sleeping child and wrapped her quickly in a blanket. He put her teddy-bear on top, and staggered out of the room. He went downstairs and put the child on a sofa. She woke up, frightened, and he gave her the teddy-bear.

"Stay there with teddy," he said. "I'll fetch your mummy."

But there seemed to be no one in the house at all! Jack felt he hadn't time to look far. That room would be burnt to bits whilst he hunted for someone! There was just a chance he might put out the fire before it got a real hold.

He tore upstairs again. The first thing he saw when he got to the room was a canary in a cage. It was half suffocated with smoke. He unhooked the cage and

put it outside the door. He saw a pail standing nearby and he took it to the bathroom. He filled it with water as quickly as he could, put the plug in the bath, left the taps running to fill the bath, and carried the pail to the burning room.

Swish! Sizzle-sizzle! He flung the water over the burning curtains and basket. The flames spat at him and disappeared. But the rug was still burning and the flames had caught the table now, too. Back he went to the bathroom and filled his pail again.

Swish! Slish-slosh! Sizzle!

Out went the flames on the rug, and the table stopped burning. Back went Jack for more water. Another three pails and the fire went out altogether.

Just as he was throwing the very last pail of water on the floor there came the sound of footsteps up the stairs. The mother and father had at last come in from the garden and had heard the strange noises upstairs.

"*What* are you doing here?" roared the father.

"Oh, sir, I couldn't find anyone, and this room was on fire," panted Jack,

157

tired with carrying heavy pails of water.
"I saw the fire from the road below and
I came in at the front door. I yelled and
yelled, but –"

"Where's little Ruth?" suddenly cried
the mother. "Where's my little Ruth?
Oh, what's happened to her?"

"I carried her downstairs," said Jack.
"She's all right. She's got her teddy.
Then I came back to put out the fire.
I'm afraid I couldn't save the curtains or
the table – but most of the room's all
right. It would all have gone up in
flames, though, in another five
minutes."

The mother rushed downstairs to her
little girl. Ruth was fast asleep on the
sofa, cuddling her teddy-bear, wrapped
warmly in a blanket.

"Where's the canary?" said the father.

"I unhooked the cage. It's out there
somewhere," said Jack. "I say, sir, this
room's an awful mess with water – but I
did the best thing I could think of."

"Look here, my boy, I can't thank you
enough," said the man, putting his arm

round Jack. "You're a marvel. In fact, you're a hero!"

Jack laughed. "Wish I was, sir. But I'm not. Any boy would have done the same. Any girl, too. It just happened that I came by at the right moment."

What a fuss the parents made of Jack! Ruth's grandmother was called in when she came back from the post, and she marvelled at Jack, too. She brought him the largest piece of chocolate cake he had ever seen in his life. He was pleased.

"And now I'm going into my study to write," said the man. "I'm somebody who writes for the papers, Jack. Ah, you didn't know that! Well, you tell your mother and father to look on page one of their newspaper tomorrow morning. They'll be proud to read what's there!"

159

Now, the next morning two mothers opened their newspapers. One was the mother of Paul and one was the mother of Jack.

"Now, you'll see there's nothing at all about a fire," said Paul's mother to him. "I expect it was all your imagination, seeing a fire at the house at the corner, Paul."

And what *did* she see when she opened the paper? This is what she saw:

THE BOY WHO CAME BY

He came by my house last night, this boy. He saw the glow of a room on fire. Did he run away in fright? No. Did he stand and do nothing? No. He went in. He ran up to the room. He rescued my

160

little girl in her cot. He unhooked the canary cage. He fetched pails of water and he put out the fire all by himself. What a boy!

Jack Brown, we're proud of you. And you'll be proud of the medal you'll get, and the gold watch that is coming to you.

And your parents will be proud of *you*!

Well done, Jack Brown.

That is what Paul and his mother read. What do you suppose they felt?

And that is what Jack's father and mother read, too. They couldn't believe their eyes, because Jack hadn't said a word. Their Jack! Look at his name in the paper! He was a hero.

"Oh, Jack – I'm so PROUD of you!" said his mother.

"Well done Jack, well done," said his father, red with pride.

Well, I've told you the story of the two children who came by the house at the corner that night. One might well have been you. Which would you have been, I wonder – Paul or Jack?

The Boy
Who Kicked

"I don't want Mike to come to tea with me," said Anne, when her mother said she might ask Mike that very afternoon.

"Why not?" said her mother in surprise.

"Because he kicks," said Anne. So Mike was not asked to tea. It was quite true – he did kick. He had begun kicking when he was three years old and didn't get what he wanted. He just kicked out with his hard little shoes, and hurt people!

Well, usually children stop kicking when they are four or five, but Mike didn't. Whenever he was cross, he kicked! He kicked a good many people and children. He kicked his mother when she scolded him. He kicked his sister when she wanted a toy he was playing with. He kicked the boys at school when they displeased him, and once he even kicked his school-teacher!

She sent him home with a note. "Michael is too fond of kicking. Will you please make him understand that we do not allow such habits? He is seven now, and he may hurt someone badly."

His mother was disgusted with him. "Mike, I really am ashamed of you. You have a kind father and mother, a lovely home, a dear little sister, plenty of toys, heaps of love and kindness – and yet you have this dreadful way of kicking

and hurting people as soon as you don't get exactly what you want! You MUST stop kicking. Now, go straight back to school and tell your teacher you are sorry, and promise faithfully never to do such a thing again."

Mike looked sulky. He didn't want to do that. He didn't like saying he was sorry. But he saw that his mother looked very stern, and he was afraid she might tell his father if he didn't go at once. So he went out of the house, banged the front door, and ran down the path.

He kicked hard at the stones on the road as he went. He kicked at the kerb. He really was in a very bad temper.

He climbed over a stile to cross the field that led to the school. Halfway down the path he met a sturdy little man, carrying a big sack. The path was narrow, and Mike didn't see why he should get out of the way. Let the man go off the path. *He* wasn't going to!

The man stopped and looked in surprise at the frowning boy. "Make way," he said. "Get off the path and let

me pass with my heavy load."

"*You* get off," said Mike, rudely. The man looked even more surprised. He put down his sack and stood squarely in the middle of the path.

"Now," he said quietly. "Move yourself, my lad!"

Mike tried to push rudely past. The man caught hold of his arm and held him.

"Not so fast, not so fast!" he said. "You are going to do what you are told, my boy!"

Then, of course, Mike kicked out at him. He kicked the man hard on the leg, thinking that he would at once let him go. But the man didn't.

"You're kicking the wrong one this time," he said softly. "You didn't know I was Williwink the Wizard, did you? Well, I am! Donkeys kick – you should be a donkey, a dear little donkey, with long ears and a tail, and legs that kick! And what is more, you *shall* be a little donkey, my boy. Yes, you *shall!*"

He let go Mike's arm, picked up his sack, and went on his way. Mike found himself pushed off the path, and he stared angrily round. He felt his ears twitching – and, dear me, what was that swinging to and fro behind him? He

turned his head to look – and, my goodness me, he saw a donkey's broad grey back, finished off with a long, swinging tail!

"I'm a donkey!" he said. "That man must have been a wizard, as he said! He's turned me into a kicking donkey! Whatever shall I do?"

He tried to run after the man. It was strange to have four feet to run on instead of two. Mike wasn't used to it, and he fell over. By the time he got up again the man had disappeared. Mike didn't know what to do.

He was suddenly very frightened. Everything seemed strange. His head felt heavy. His ears felt too long. He didn't like having a tail. He opened his mouth to let out a wail.

"Eee-aw, EEE-AW!" said his mouth, and this extraordinary noise frightened poor Mike so much that he galloped down the path, jumped clean over the stile, and went home as fast as ever he could.

"I must get back to mother," he

thought. "She will put things right. She always does."

He came to his house. He opened the gate with his nose and trotted up the path. He banged on the door with his front hoof.

Mary, the daily help, opened it. She gave a shout of surprise when she saw the donkey, and rushed indoors. Mike followed her, and cantered down the hall. He pushed open the sitting-room door and looked inside. His mother was there, sewing.

He trotted up to her, and put his big head on her shoulder. She dropped her sewing, and screamed.

"A donkey! Get away, you great thing! How dare you come into the house like this? What do you mean by breathing all over me like that and putting your big head on my shoulder? Get away, I tell you."

Mike tried to tell his mother that he was really her little boy and not a donkey, but all he could say was "EEE-aw, ee-aw" over and over again. His mother could not bear the noise. She took up the poker and gave Mike a sharp tap with it on his broad back.

"Get along out with you! And don't you come indoors again! Go back to where you belong!"

Mike tried to say that this was where he belonged. He was hustled out of the room, down the hall and out of the door. His mother took a walking-stick from the hall-stand and gave the poor donkey a good whack.

"Now you'll know what you'll get if you come into a house again," she said. "Spoiling my lovely polished hall and frightening me like that!"

Mike did not dare to go back again. He went into a nearby field and wandered sadly about, thinking of dinnertime, and the good smell that had come out of the kitchen. He saw Mandy, his little sister, go skipping up the path, home from school.

He went into the front garden after a while, and looked in at the window. His mother and Mandy were sitting at the table, eating a good dinner. It did look so nice. His mother looked up, and saw him peeping in at the window.

"There's that donkey again!" she cried. "Hi, Harry! Turn that donkey out of the garden, please."

Harry was the gardener. He was sitting in the shed eating his dinner. He jumped up at once and went to Mike. Mike kicked him!

"Oooh! Ow!" yelled the gardener. "You bad-tempered creature! Where's my stick? Donkeys that kick must be whacked!"

He gave poor Mike a big whack. Mike trotted out of the gate and stood in the field, crying big tears down his long grey nose. He was hungry and very frightened, and unhappy. To think this had happened just because he kicked someone!

He did not dare to go into the garden again, because Harry was on the watch for him. When night came he was more

171

miserable than ever. He knew his mother must be worried because he hadn't come home – but if he did try to go home she would only drive him away! He wanted a good meal. The grass tasted funny. He wanted a good drink. The stream looked dirty. He wanted his own comfortable little bed. The field was hard and cold to lie on.

"Hallo!" said a voice, making him jump. "Here is the little donkey again! Are you enjoying being able to kick whenever you like, grey donkey?"

Mike shook his head. He could just see Williwink beside him in the twilit field. How he wished he had a boy's tongue so that he could ask him to change him back into his own shape again!

"I want a grey donkey to ride to the market and back," said Williwink. "I've a good mind to take you and keep you. But I suppose I must give you another chance. I am always giving people chances, and *sometimes* they deserve them and sometimes they don't.

Well – I'll give you *your* chance – but mind, if I find you don't deserve it, I'll change you back into a kicking donkey again as sure as you've got a tail!"

He gave Mike a light blow on the back. The boy felt a change come over him at once. He was smaller and lighter. He had two legs instead of four. He had arms and hands, and his ears felt neat and small. He could no longer twitch them. And that horrid long tail was gone.

"Thank you," he said humbly to Williwink. "I'm sorry I kicked you. I promise I'll deserve my chance."

He ran home as fast as he could. He found the front door open, for his mother had been anxiously looking out for him. He ran indoors and found her with Mandy. They were so glad and so surprised to see him.

He flung his arms round them both and gave them such a loving hug that they were really astonished. It wasn't like Mike to be so nice!

"Mother! I was that grey donkey!" he cried, and he told his mother and Mandy the whole story. They could hardly believe it was true.

"Oh, Mike, don't ever kick again, will you?" begged Mandy. "I don't want you to be a donkey, I don't, I don't!"

That was six months ago, children, and Mike is still a boy and not a donkey. I think he must have learnt his lesson, don't you?

It Came Back
to Him in the End

It all began when Tom did a bad and foolish thing. He was sitting on the bus stop seat with two boys, waiting for the bus to take him home.

On the other end of the seat was old Mrs Trent, nodding her head, almost asleep, as she waited for the bus, too. Beside her was a full basket of shopping.

One of the boys nudged Tom. "I say, look – do you see what the old lady has got at the top of her basket?"

Tom looked. Mrs Trent had bought a bar of chocolate cream for her grandson, and there it was, at the very top of the basket.

"Take it," whispered the boy to Tom. "She's asleep and she won't know. I dare you to!"

Now dares are silly, of course – they are always meant to make you do bad or dangerous things, and you have to be very brave and wise to say no.

Tom wasn't wise, nor was he brave enough to say he wouldn't take the dare. So he edged up slowly to old Mrs Trent, hoping that the bus would come before he could do such a bad thing. Tom wasn't really bad. He just wanted to show the other boys that he was daring enough to do what they said.

He put his hand into the basket. His fingers closed over the bar of chocolate. He lifted it out gently. And then something happened.

176

A big dog came bounding up and knocked against him playfully. The chocolate flew out of his hand and landed on the ground. The dog pounced on it at once!

It cracked the bar in half, paper and all – and at that very moment, when the dog had the chocolate bar in his mouth, old Mrs Trent woke up! She saw the dog eating her precious bar of chocolate and was very angry indeed.

She picked up her umbrella and began to whip the dog. Biff, biff, whack! Biff! WHACK!

177

The dog yelped in pain. The three boys looked on in horror. Tom was as red as a beetroot. It was all his fault that the dog was being beaten; but although he had been bold enough to do what the other boys had dared him to, he wasn't brave enough to own up. So he just watched whilst the dog was beaten.

Ah, Tom – you've started a horrid chain of happenings that will come back to you in the end. You wait and see!

Up came the owner of the dog, a little fierce-eyed woman. "How dare you beat my dog like that! Put your umbrella down at once, I tell you! The poor creature, you've almost broken its back. It's a wonder he didn't fly at you."

"He stole a chocolate bar out of my basket!" cried Mrs Trent. "He's a thief-dog! Taking things out of people's baskets!"

"I'm sure he never did," said the other woman, patting her dog gently. "He has never stolen anything in his life. Never! You just say you're sorry for beating my

dog or I'll do something to *make* you sorry."

"I'm not apologising to a dog, so there!" said old Mrs Trent, gathering up her things as she saw the bus coming. "And, what's more, you can't make me *feel* sorry, either!"

"Oh, can't I!" called the other woman as Mrs Trent got on the bus. "Well, I can! You get the fish-scraps for your cat from my shop, don't you? Well, you won't get any more!"

179

You see, she was Mrs Kipps, who kept the only fish shop in the village. Every other day she packed up a nice little parcel of fish-scraps for Mrs Trent's big tabby-cat, and Mrs Trent fetched them. The cat loved the scraps and always waited impatiently for them to be cooked.

Mrs Kipps turned to the three boys, who were just getting on the bus, too. "I'll teach her to say my dog steals!" she cried. "Why, she'll be saying next that *you* steal!"

That made Tom go redder than ever. He was really ashamed of himself. So were the other boys. But the thing was done, and hadn't been put right by Tom when it could have been.

Mrs Kipps was as good as her word. She gave all her fish-scraps to Mr Morris for his Siamese cats. There wasn't a scrap for Mrs Trent when she called.

"I told you I'd not save you any more because you beat my dear old dog," said Mrs Kipps firmly. "You can buy good fish for your cat from now on. Instead of ten pennyworth of scraps you'll have to buy fifty pence worth of fish."

"I can't afford it," said Mrs Trent. "You know I can't."

"You should have thought of that before you beat my dog and called him a thief," said Mrs Kipps. "Next customer, please."

Well, Mrs Trent went home without her usual fish-scraps. Her tabby-cat met her at the door and was surprised not to smell fish. It mewed loudly.

"None for you today, poor puss," said Mrs Trent. "I'll give you what tit-bits I can from my own food, but it won't be much! You'll have to do a little hunting on your own and feed yourself."

The cat waited about for the fish, but it got none because there was none to get. Mrs Trent put down bits and pieces, but the cat was a large one and was always hungry. It grew thin and starved-looking, and hunted about in the rubbish-heaps for food.

Then it smelt at the dustbins. People put all kinds of things in there, the cat knew that. If only it could move the lids it could get into the bins and scrape about for odds and ends of food.

Well, it was a big cat and a clever one. It soon learnt how to shift the dustbin lids. Crash! They would fall to the ground and then the cat would leap nimbly into the bin and sniff about

for odd scraps.

Now one day a rat came to the district. It was a big one, but rather thin, because it had not found much food the last week or two. It smelt the cat and was afraid. It hid under the floor of a garden shed one night, after it had smelt the cat around, and listened to find out where the cat lived. The rat didn't want to live anywhere near it.

And then the rat found out that the cat went round the dustbins, jerking off

the lids and eating the scraps inside. The rat was pleased.

"I've never been able to move a dustbin lid," he thought. "This is grand! I'll wait till the cat leaves one dustbin and goes to the next, and then I'll pop into each one after her, as soon as she's gone, and finish up what she's left!"

Well, that is exactly what he did, and before long he became very plump and well-fed indeed. Each night he followed the cat around at a safe distance, feeding from the dustbins whose lids she had taken off.

Now the rat began to think it would

184

be a very good idea to take a rat wife for himself and have some young rats. "I could always find plenty of food for them in the dustbins," he thought. "Yes, I'll go and find a nice young rat and ask her to be my wife."

So very soon another rat came to join him and made a cosy nest of paper and wood shavings under the floor of the garden shed.

Ten young rats were born, all lively and strong. The big rat was pleased, and so was his wife. "Soon we shall cover this district with rats," said he. "Nobody likes us, but I don't care! As long as the cat takes off the dustbin lids for us we are all right for food."

But soon people grew tired of hearing the crash of dustbin lids in the night, and they set a watch for the cat. Mr Wilton caught it and looked at it.

"It's Mrs Trent's cat! She must lock it in the house at night. We can't have it taking off our dustbin lids and scraping about in the rubbish each night. It just won't do!"

So Mrs Trent had to keep her old cat in the house at night – and there was no more crashing of dustbin lids at midnight and no more stealing of dustbin food!

And that meant that the rat couldn't find the food either! He was surprised and annoyed when he found all the dustbin lids on at night. No more scraps for him. No more tit-bits for his wife and children either.

"It's no good asking the cat why it doesn't go round the bins at night any more," he told his wife. "It would just snap me up. Cats are like that!"

"Well, you will have to go round and

see what you can find," said his wife.
"We've ten children now and it will be
hard to feed them. Hunt well."

The rat hunted all night long, but all
he found were a few crumbs of biscuit
dropped by a child, and an old potato
skin.

"This won't do for our large family!"
said his wife. "You must do better than
this! Are there no young chicks or
ducklings you can find? There are often
plenty at this time of year. Go to the
farm and see."

Now Tom's father kept a farm not far
off. Tom loved the farm. He loved all
the animals on it – the horses, the cows,
the sheep, the ducks, the pigs, and even
the old turkeys that said "gobble,
gobble" in deep voices whenever he
passed.

This year he had ten little yellow
ducklings of his own – dear little things
a few days old, hatched out by an old
mother hen. She had the ten ducklings
in a coop with her and kept guard over
them day and night.

And one night the rat smelt them out! He crept up and put his nose between the bars of the coop. The mother hen pecked it at once and he drew back.

"Cheep," said a duckling, and put its head out from beneath the hen's wing.

"Cluck," said the hen warningly, and the duckling drew it back. But the rat had seen it!

He went back home to his wife. "There are ducklings at the farm, with a silly hen to keep watch," he said. "I'll soon have them!"

He was sly and cunning. He found a tiny hole at the back of the coop and gnawed away at it till he had made it big

188

enough to slip through. The mother hen did not hear anything. The rat saw a tiny webbed foot sticking out from under the hen's feathers and pounced on it. With a frightened cheep the duckling awoke - but before the hen could do anything the rat had gone off with the duckling!

He came back for another that night, and yet another. The hen clucked and squawked, but the rat was too clever for her.

Now when Tom went to see his ducklings the next day there were only seven. He was very upset. What could have happened to the others? Had a rat got them? He would move the coop to another place!

But the rat soon found out where the coop had been moved to, and a night or two later he went to the mother hen again. She was awake at once. She clucked loudly and turned herself round to peck at him.

In a flash, the rat was round at the front of the coop, in between the bars, before the hen had even had time to turn herself round! He dragged out a cheeping duckling, and went back for another. He got a peck on the back, but he didn't mind that. He carried off the ducklings, and his wife was full of delight.

By the end of the week not a single duckling was left, not one. The rat had had them all. Tom went to his mother with tears in his eyes.

"There are none left now," he told her. "Oh, Mother, I do feel so miserable. They were such lovely ducklings, and I was going to let them grow into beautiful big ducks and lay eggs for me to sell. They would be my very own."

"It's a shame, Tom," said his mother.

"It's not fair," said Tom. "What have I done to have such a horrid thing happen to me? I haven't done anything at all!"

Oh, but you have, Tom! Have you forgotten when you were dared to take that bar of chocolate out of old Mrs Trent's basket? Have you forgotten how she beat Mrs Kipp's dog for stealing it and you didn't say a word? You didn't guess that because of that Mrs Kipps wouldn't save her fish-scraps for Mrs Trent's cat, and so her cat learnt to push off dustbin lids and look for scraps. You didn't know that a rat came and

191

helped himself to scraps, too, from the dustbins and took a wife and raised a hungry family.

You didn't guess that when the cat was locked up at night and couldn't take off the dustbin lids the rat went looking elsewhere for food, and found your dear little ducklings. It was all because of something *you* did, Tom, that your ducklings were stolen and killed.

Poor Tom! I feel sorry for him, don't you? He really didn't know that one wrong deed will set a whole lot of other wrongs going round the world, and will often come back to the one who starts them. Well – I'm going to be very, very careful – aren't you? I think I'll set a good deed going, not a bad one!